GARAVI GUJARAT
2020, BEAVER RUIN ROAD,
NORCROSS, GA 30071
TEL: 770 263 7728
Email: usa@gg2.net

SPIRIT OF IRON

Janice Jordan Shefelman

Illustrated by
Tom · Karl · Dan Shefelman

Eakin Press · Austin, Texas

FIRST EDITION

Published in the United States of America
By Eakin Press, P.O. Drawer 90159, Austin, Texas 78709-0159

ISBN 0-89015-636-0 — Hardback
ISBN 0-89015-889-4 — Paperback

Library of Congress Cataloging-in-Publication Data

Shefelman, Janice Jordan.
  Spirit of iron.

  Bibliography: p.
  Includes glossary.
  Summary: In mid-nineteenth-century Texas, Mina Jordan turns fifteen, but she is not ready to become the young lady everyone expects her to be.
  [1. Frontier and Pioneer life — Fiction. 2. Texas — Fiction] I. Shefelman, Tom, ill. II. Shefelman, Dan, ill. IV. Title.
PZ7.S54115Sp 1987 [Fic] 87-13395
ISBN 0-89015-636-0

For Mother
who has the spirit

AUTHOR'S NOTE

My first two books about Mina and her family, *A Paradise Called Texas* and *Willow Creek Home,* are based on the experiences of my German ancestors who immigrated to Texas in 1845. There was a real girl, Johanne Ernestine Wilhelmine Jordan, who was called Mina for short. Her father was my great-grandfather.

As I wrote those books, Mina became very much alive in my mind. So alive, in fact, that she clamored for another story — an adventure story to take her far from the cabin on Willow Creek. That is how *Spirit of Iron* came to be written. Her adventures in this book are fictional, but they could have happened.

CONTENTS

v

"Through fire is the spirit forged."
Katherine Paterson
The Sign of the Chrysanthemum

1

A Gallop

Mina galloped along Willow Creek on Tucan. Her long, blonde hair flew behind her like a mane as they moved in rhythm together, girl and horse, pounding the sandy road. She bent low over Tucan's neck and saw only a blur of the passing trees from the corners of her eyes.

There was something still wild about this black horse when they galloped together. He seemed to be running with his brother and sister Mustangs again, racing across the Texas plains before the Comanches captured him. Mina felt that same wild freedom seep into her as she rode. The wind of their speed swept across her face and tugged at the long skirts that billowed around her legs.

Tante Lisette, her new mother, always said, *Wilhelmine Jordan, you ride like a wild Indian.* And now, since Mina had turned fifteen, *Tante* had begun to say it was not ladylike, that she must ride sidesaddle. Not only that, she said it was time Mina began sewing her dowry.

Papa had bought her a new sidesaddle, but she preferred to use her old one or to ride bareback as she did on these early mornings. She would rather ride Tucan across country with the wind in her hair than sit at home sewing her dowry. If only Papa would take her with him on his long hauling trips to Fredericksburg or Austin. But it was the men and boys who got to do that. Women had to stay home.

Nearing Little Creek, Mina crouched forward, clutching Tucan's mane as she loosened his reins. He stretched his neck out, hesitating for a moment to look at the creek. She gave him a gentle nudge with her heels, and he jumped. For just a moment she lost her seat, but she gripped with her legs and held tight to his mane as they landed on the other side.

She collected the reins and rode on, past the big live-oak and the log schoolhouse, past the von Trappe cabin on the other side of the creek and the Dannheims' close by the road, to a hill on the right where she usually turned around and headed back home. The sun was climbing higher behind the willows and pecan trees.

Tucan slowed his gait and looked back at her as if to say, *Shouldn't we turn back?*

"We *should*," Mina said aloud, patting his shiny black neck, "but let's ride to the top of the hill."

From there she would be able to look out toward the Lipan Apache village on the Llano River where her friend, Amaya, lived. Mina had not seen her since the Lipans left in the fall to follow the buffalo herds. Amaya must be back now, Mina thought, for they always returned in time to plant.

Tucan stepped his way up the crumbling limestone ledges to the top. Looking to the south she saw plumes of

smoke rising from the wide river valley — smoke that surely came from the village.

"Let's ride over and pay Amaya a visit. Would you like that, Tucan?"

Tucan tossed his head.

She had ridden this way many times to visit Amaya. Once the two girls pricked their thumbs with a thorn and then pressed them together in a secret pact of blood sisters. Sometimes Mina wished she were truly Amaya's sister and could go on the long, wandering buffalo hunts. It would be better than staying at home, sewing a dowry.

The tepees were clustered along the river, some twenty of them. A group of boys played with their toy bows in a grassy meadow nearby. They seemed to be stalking an imaginary herd of buffalo. Women were busy gathering wood and bringing water from the river. Some were already at work in the vegetable garden. They all stopped to watch as she approached. Some waved, recognizing her by the horse she rode and her blonde hair.

Mina waved back, looking for Amaya among them. Then she saw her carrying a pitch basket of water. Amaya set it down and ran to meet Mina, her long, black hair streaming behind her.

"Mina!" she called.

Mina dismounted. The two girls stood looking at each other but not touching, for the Lipans did not show affection in public.

"I have happiness to see you," Amaya said in Spanish, the language of their friendship. Her dark eyes were soft, and she tilted her head to one side, smiling. Rings of copper wire strung with beads hung from her ears, and she wore a fringed doeskin dress and leggings. No one would guess by looking at her delicate features and slim figure that she could ride and shoot as well as any warrior in the village. Her father often took her along on the hunt.

"I also have happiness," Mina answered in Spanish. She had not seen Amaya for six months, and yet it was as if they had never been apart. "When you return to *Río* Llano?"

Amaya thought a moment. "When this moon new." Then she motioned to Mina. "Come, we go in tepee. My father and mother want see you. They like Girl-With-Hair-Like-Sun."

Amaya led the way to her tepee, picking up the pitch basket of water as she went. Her father, Custaleta, was chief of this band of Lipans. Their tepee was the largest in the village. Painted on it in bright colors were scenes of his brave deeds.

Mina staked Tucan and followed Amaya inside. Chief Custaleta sat cross-legged on the far side of the fire, restringing his bow. His hair was cut short over his left ear, where he wore four copper earrings. On the

4

right, his long black braid was doubled up and tied with red strings. Mina saw that the locks of her blonde hair still decorated his braid, though they had grown somewhat dingy.

"Welcome to friend of my daughter," he said in Spanish, his face immobile. He laid the bow across his lap and motioned her to the left of the fire. Wapako, his round-faced wife, knelt before the fire where she had placed small cakes in the ashes to cook.

Mina nodded her thanks and sat down with Amaya in silence. No one spoke. This Indian courtesy of silence no longer made Mina uncomfortable. She had come to think of it as a time to sense the feelings of others and compose her thoughts. She watched the small flame dancing on top of a log, remembering that first time she met Custaleta, Wapako, and Amaya.

It was on her eleventh birthday. She had wandered away from the cabin searching for acorns to grind for bread since they had no corn or wheat. On the banks of Comal Creek she happened upon the Indians, and, being frightened, she dropped all the acorns from her apron. But Custaleta did not want her scalp as she feared. He wanted only some locks of her hair. In exchange Amaya gave her a blue beaded belt and helped her pick up the acorns. They had been friends ever since. A feeling of warmth for this family flooded over Mina, and she felt herself smiling.

Wapako picked up one of the cakes, brushed it off, and handed it to Mina. She took a bite. The ashcake was heavy and dry, but sweet with honey.

"How your father?" Chief Custaleta asked.

"My father *muy bien, gracias.*"

"No more trouble from Comanche?"

5

Mina shook her head. "We no see Comanche for many months . . . moons," she answered.

"*Bueno*. I hope never see again."

They all laughed.

Custaleta talked of the buffalo hunt and how his son, Nakona, had killed two with one arrow. So great was the force of his shot that the arrow had passed through one of the beasts and into another.

"Now he paint on tepee. Someday be chief."

Mina could listen to his stories all day, but it was growing late.

"My father have anger if I not return home now." She thanked Wapako for the ashcake and said farewell to Custaleta.

"You come again," Wapako said, smiling kindly.

"I come," Mina assured her.

Outside the tepee Mina saw that the sun had risen high above the treetops. If she did not hurry, Papa would ride out looking for her.

"When you come to Willow Creek?" Mina asked Amaya as she mounted Tucan.

"Soon." Amaya raised her hand and made the sign for *sister* by putting her hand to her hair and then two fingers to her lips. "Soon we see again."

2

A Quarrel

By the time Mina came in sight of the cabin on a rise above Willow Creek, the sun was halfway up the sky. Smoke rose from the Jordans' chimney and from the Kaufmanns' across the creek where Anna lived. She could not see the Hesslers' cabin from here, but a thin plume of smoke arose from that direction, a mile or so away.

Papa was at work in the cornfield, guiding the plow behind the yoke of oxen. He always said, *Work makes life sweet.* If that was true, their lives must be sweeter than honey, for it seemed to Mina that all they did was work. Maybe when she was older she would understand what Papa meant. But for now, what made life sweet for her was Daniel Hessler, Tucan, and her dreams of adventure.

As she came alongside the rail fence Mina called, *"Guten Morgen,* Papa," as cheerfully as she could. Though she could speak English now, she still spoke German at home and with the other families along Willow Creek.

Papa looked up. *"Guten Morgen,* Mina, or is it *guten Tag?"* He laid down the plow and came toward the fence.

Mina dismounted and held Tucan's reins in her hand, waiting.

Papa took off his hat and wiped his forehead on his sleeve. With a pang Mina realized that he looked older than when they left Germany five years ago to come to Texas. The beard that fringed his square jaw had gray in it now.

"Mina . . . "

"I know, Papa. I am late, and *Tante* needs me. It's just that I rode over to Custaleta's village to see if they had returned — and they had."

Papa looked at her with his big gentle eyes. "Do you think that was a wise decision?"

"No, Papa." She knew it was not right for her to be out pleasuring herself, visiting friends when the garden needed weeding, the cabin needed sweeping. There was wood to bring in, beds to be made, chickens to be fed, Liesel to be milked. She must be terribly selfish thinking only of what made her happy.

Then she brightened. "I'll work twice as fast to make up for it."

Papa nodded and went back to work. Mina led Tucan around to the well, drew some water, and poured it into the trough for him to drink. Then she hobbled him and removed the bridle.

"Even you cannot be free, Tucan." She stroked his neck, giving him a final pat.

The cabin door stood open to the warm spring morning. Peter was playing with corncobs tied to a small piece of wood, pretending they were oxen, and making trails with them through the sandy dirt. When he saw Mina coming, he raised his arms to her. He was two and a half years old now, and he had Papa's wide mouth and big eyes.

Mina took his plump, grimy little hands in hers, lifted him, and swung him around and around until they were both dizzy. As she stopped they fell to the ground together, laughing.

Tante Lisette came to the door. Her dark hair, parted in the middle, was pulled back to a braided coil. Though she was tall and slim, the baby growing inside her made a slight bulge under her apron. She smiled briefly at their play, but then disappeared into the cabin. Mina stood up quickly to get on with her chores.

At the washstand on the porch she dipped water into a basin and washed her hands. Then she emptied the basin, pouring soapy water on a trumpet vine that grew on the corner post.

As she stepped through the doorway, *Tante* said, "Mina, I don't like to scold, but . . . "

Mina turned away. She did not want to hear any more. She knew she was fifteen years old now and she knew what she had to do.

"You know, Mina," *Tante* kept on, "most girls your age have begun their dowries. Anna has."

Mina swung around to face her. "I don't *care* what Anna has done and I don't care about a dowry." The words burst out of her before she could stop them.

"Oh come now, you don't mean that."

But she *did* mean it. Even though she had loved her new mother from the start, and begged Papa to marry, *Tante* Lisette did not understand her, not the way Papa did — or used to. Lately Papa seemed to be taking *Tante's*

9

side too. He always used to say Mina had fire in her veins, but now, even he seemed to want to put it out.

Was there something wrong with her that she yearned to escape this small world of theirs? She remembered how she envied Captain Libben on the ship crossing the Atlantic. What an exciting life he had. But whoever heard of a girl being captain of a ship?

Mina picked up the broom from beside the fireplace and began to sweep furiously, stirring dust up all over the cabin.

"Mina, be calm now and act like a lady."

Mina stopped and threw down the broom.

"I don't *want* to be a lady — not ever, ever, ever. I want to be a wild Indian. Besides, you cannot tell me that. You are not my real mother."

The words hung between them in the silence of the cabin. *Tante's* mouth opened, but she did not speak. Mina turned and ran out the door. From the corners of her eyes she saw Papa stop and watch her as she ran down toward the creek. Tears spilled over from her eyes, but she did not bother to wipe them away.

It felt good to run along the sandy creek bed. She ran until she came to a large, old willow whose roots had been exposed when the creek ran high. The roots were striated like the trunk. When she sat down between them, they seemed to embrace her with rough arms. She curled up, leaning against the trunk, and broke into sobs.

So much had happened since they came to Texas, and Mina wept for it all — for Mama, who lay buried on that lonely Texas beach, for Opa, who died of pneumonia after they left him in Germany. Was it a broken heart instead? Mina wondered. She had been a little girl then —

Papa's *kleine* Mina — but now, in the spring of 1850, she was almost a woman, and she wept for that most of all.

When she had cried herself out, and her breath came in jerky gasps, she felt something furry against her arm. It was Schnurri, her gray and black striped cat. She rubbed this way and that until Mina picked her up and cradled her warm, purring body against her own.

3

Making Amends

Those hateful words, *You are not my real mother,* kept repeating over and over again in Mina's head. She had not meant them, and now she must somehow make amends. *Tante* Lisette was a good mother, and she had made Papa smile and laugh again.

Mina ran her fingers through her hair, braided it, and tied each one with a ribbon from the pocket of her denim dress. Then gathering herself up, she started back toward the cabin with Schnurri following.

Tante was feeding the chickens by the coop behind the cabin. Peter helped her, scattering corn he picked out of a bowl.

As Mina approached, *Tante* looked up. Mina could not read her expression. She did not frown or smile but looked back down at the chickens pecking the ground around her.

Mina wanted to go to *Tante* Lisette, say she was

sorry, and then they would embrace. Instead she walked on to the cabin and through the open door. She would finish the sweeping job so abruptly abandoned. But the cabin had already been neatly swept, the broom put back in place beside the hearth.

Mina took her apron from a hook, tied it on, and went outside. The small peach trees in the orchard were covered with pale pink blossoms. She inhaled their sweet fragrance. Papa had planted them three years ago, and this year they would bear fruit for the first time.

Lifting the gate rail, Mina entered the garden. She held the corners of her apron together for a bag and began to pick beans for dinner. Papa came toward her, walking the plow down the row in the adjacent cornfield. He nodded approval as he headed the oxen around and started back in the other direction. Did he remember that she was the same Mina he had taught to fire a shotgun?

At dinner and later at supper that evening, *Tante* Lisette was quiet. Mina had brought in the firewood and made the corn bread. They had spoken only the necessary words to each other in preparing supper. There was no doubt that *Tante* was deeply hurt.

During supper Peter dribbled crumbs of corn bread onto his smock. Pointing to his cup he said, "Mama do."

Tante poured some milk for him which he drank down noisily. Peter's gulping and the *ticktock* of the clock were the only sounds in the room. The air seemed tense with unspoken words.

Finally, when supper was over, Peter crawled into *Tante's* lap as Mina brought the family Bible for Papa to read.

He pulled the candle closer and opened the book to the middle. Turning a few pages, Papa found the place he wanted and said, "Proverbs sixteen, verse thirty-two."

He looked up at Mina before beginning in the deep, resounding voice he used for reading the Scriptures.

He that is slow to anger is better than the mighty; and he that ruleth his spirit than he that taketh a city.

So, the lesson this evening was to be for Mina. Papa often chose his readings according to events of the day. She wished, though, that her outburst could be forgotten and not dwelled upon any longer.

Papa continued. "And chapter twenty-one, verse twenty-three."

Whoso keepeth his mouth and his tongue keepeth his soul from troubles.

"Finally, from the book of James, chapter one, verse nineteen."

Wherefore, my beloved brethren, let every man be swift to hear, slow to speak, slow to wrath.

Mina watched Papa close the book and look at her, his eyes sad, searching.

"Do you understand the wisdom of the Holy Writ, Mina?"

"*Ja*, Papa. But I cannot be so good as that. I think I would *burst*."

A flicker of amusement appeared in Papa's eyes. "You can try, Mina. Will you apologize to *Tante* Lisette now? She was only saying what she thought Mama would have her say."

Rather than calming Mina, all this talk was stirring her up again. Abruptly she looked at *Tante* for the first time since morning. *Tante* waited for Mina's apology.

"I am sorry," Mina blurted.

Tante Lisette smiled, then got up and handed Peter

15

to Papa. Coming over to Mina, she hugged her around the shoulders.

"All is forgiven, Mina."

Mina tensed. She wanted to bolt out of the room, jump on Tucan, and ride like a wild Indian.

Instead, she excused herself from the table, said good night, and took a candle up the ladder to her room in the loft.

The soft light flickered on the writing table under the open window. Mina pulled her brown denim dress over her head and stepped out of her petticoat. Then, removing her vest and drawers, she slipped into her white night dress.

No sooner had she sat down at the table than she heard Schnurri meowing from outside on the roof, wanting in as usual. She reached out the window and Schnurri came into her hand. Drawing her inside carefully, she stroked her purring body and set her on the small pillow under the eave. It was low and snug there, and the cat curled up to sleep. Mina liked having another living thing in the loft with her. The candle seemed a live thing too, and Mina sat down again at the table.

Johanna, her doll with a china head, sat on the table, propped against the wall, smiling sweetly as always. Her cheeks were painted with rosy circles, and her eyes were shiny black and merry. She had come all the way across the Atlantic Ocean with Mina, and never once stopped smiling.

On the other corner of the writing table, Mina had placed her three books — her treasured library — all bought by Papa on his hauling trips. There were two school readers and her journal. She longed for other books to read, but they were too dear in Texas.

Often Mina brought the family Bible up to her loft.

That pleased Papa, for he supposed she was learning about God. But Mina read the Bible for adventure. There was the story of David standing up to the giant Goliath, with only a slingshot in his hand, and Joseph interpreting Pharoah's dreams and becoming governor over all Egypt. These stories thrilled her, and many nights she sat at the table reading until the candle burned down.

Against the opposite wall stood Mina's bed. She could lie there and look down into the room below through the square opening in the loft floor. The bed was covered with a blue embroidered coverlet that Mama had made during the long ocean crossing. It was to be part of her dowry.

Mina opened her journal to the first page, where she had written so carefully:

The Journal of

Johanne Ernestine Wilhelmine Jordan

(Mina for Short)

She looked through the pages from years past, stopping to read:

Tuesday, October 23, 1849

Chief Custaleta and his band of Lipan Apaches stopped by here today. They are leaving their camp on the Llano to follow the buffalo. Amaya said they will be back next spring. I hope so, for we have become even better friends now that I

*have learned to speak some Spanish words. Amaya wants me
to teach her English.*

*If only the Comanches were as friendly as the Lipans, there
would be no Indian troubles here. But they are not, and I suppose they never will be.*

That was last year. The Lipans had come back just as
Amaya promised.

Mina turned some more pages and came to this re-
cent entry:

Saturday, February 9, 1850

*Papa came home today from a hauling trip to Austin. My
heart fairly burst with joy. Peter was shy at first.*

*He brought news of our friend, William Allen. Papa says he
has quit surveying and has joined the Texas Rangers again.
I hope one day he will pass this way and stop for a visit. He
always has such stories to tell.*

If only girls could join the Rangers.

Mina sighed and turned to the place marked with a
red satin ribbon and began to write:

Monday, April 17, 1850

*Today I rode over to Custaleta's village. To my great joy they
have returned. One day, I fear, they will wander farther and
farther away, and I will never see Amaya again.*

But later, to my shame, I spoke without thinking to Tante
Lisette, *and we quarreled. Sometimes I think Tucan is the
only one who understands the fire that burns inside me. Well,
perhaps my dear Papa does, but* Tante *Lisette does not understand anything at all. She is such a perfect lady. Though
I love her, I cannot be like her. How am I to be then?*

Schnurri stretched and came to curl around her legs.
Mina picked her up and climbed down the ladder.

The fire had been banked, and everyone was in bed.

18

Papa and *Tante* were sleeping in their room, and Peter was over in the corner. She tiptoed to the door, lifted the latch slowly, carefully, and stepped outside. Schnurri scampered off in the direction of the creek. Mina stood for a moment at the edge of the porch, looking out at the clear night.

Whip-will, whip-will, came the call of a night bird.

She looked up at the stars. Everything was still. No breeze stirred at all. Mina felt she was standing at the edge of something about to happen.

4

Daniel

Six German families lived in cabins scattered along Willow Creek for about three miles. From her loft window the only one Mina could see was the Kaufmann cabin directly across the creek. Farther north and away from the creek was the Hessler cabin where Daniel lived.

This morning Daniel Hessler was leaving for Fredericksburg — forty miles away — to buy supplies for all the families. Mina had taken special care in combing and braiding her hair and tying it with fresh blue ribbons. She wore a clean work dress of blue and white sprigged calico.

Ever since their families had come to Willow Creek together, she had been sweet on Daniel Hessler, and he seemed to feel the same about her. At one time she had made up her mind that he was her future intended. But now she was not sure she wanted to marry anyone —

ever. Still, when he was around, Mina could think of nothing else but Daniel.

As she drew water from the well, filled the two buckets, and carried them up to the washpot, she listened for the first sound of Daniel's wagon. How she envied him. If only she could go along to Fredericksburg, but Papa had already said *nein*. Mina lowered the buckets to the ground and lifted the yoke from her shoulders. After pouring water into the washpot, she started back toward the well.

Papa was splitting logs near the old liveoak tree. The solid thud of his mallet hitting the wedge sounded again and again. Peter played in the wagon parked beside the cabin. He danced about, swinging a piece of rope.

Mina set the buckets down and climbed up into the wagon with him.

"Come, Peter, sit here." She patted the spring seat, and he sat beside her.

"Mina do." He handed her the piece of rope.

21

"Get up there, Hans and Willi," Mina shouted at the imaginary oxen. Peter squealed, jumping up and down.

"No, Peter, you must not stand up in the wagon. Sit down now and drive, because you are going to Fredericksburg." She gave him the rope again and climbed out.

His face became pouty. "No! Mina play."

"I'll be back, Peter. I have one more trip to the well."

Tante came out of the cabin carrying a firescoop of hot coals to start the fire under the washpot.

Mina drew the water slowly, dreamily, until she heard the first rattling of the wagon from across the creek. Then hurriedly, hand over hand, she pulled up the heavy bucket and emptied it. Shouldering the yoke, she walked as fast as she could back to the washing tree. Water sloshed out onto her legs.

"Gee, gee," Daniel yelled at the oxen. Mina's heart leaped as she heard his voice. Quickly pouring the water into the pot, she looked at *Tante,* asking permission with her eyes to run and meet him. *Tante* smiled and nodded yes.

Mina ran down the slope and across the road to the embankment above the creek. There she stopped, waving, as Daniel drove the oxen across the shallow flow of water that wound through the wide sandy bed.

Daniel waved back. *"Wie geht's?"*

Mina put her hands on her hips and watched him. His hair shone golden in the morning sun, and, at eighteen, he was man-grown.

"I guess you think you're a real man, going off by yourself, Daniel Hessler."

"Jawohl!" A grin spread over his face. "Want to come along?"

He was teasing her. He knew perfectly well Papa would not let her go.

"Why would I want to go anywhere with you when I can wash clothes instead?" Mina enjoyed this bantering with Daniel.

He threw back his head and laughed. She had gotten the better of him with words, but he was the one going to Fredericksburg — not Mina.

The oxen stopped at the embankment. Daniel cracked the whip over their heads to urge them on, and, Mina expected, to impress her. His bare arms were brown and muscular. She was momentarily dazzled by him.

Up on the road Daniel called, "Whoa." When the oxen stopped he jumped out of the wagon and stood beside Mina.

"So, it's washday, *Fräulein?*"

Mina did not answer. She turned, flinging her braids about, and started toward the cabin. Daniel followed her.

"I'm only teasing, Mina."

She kept on walking. She did not want him to see the tears starting in her eyes. It was foolish to cry about such a little thing. Mina wiped away the tears with the corner of her apron and took a deep breath to calm herself.

When Papa saw them he lay down his mallet and came to the cabin.

"*Guten Morgen,* Daniel."

"*Wie geht's, Herr* Jordan?"

"Well, you have a good day to travel."

"*Ja,* if only the oxen thought so."

Tante joined them with Peter in hand and greeted Daniel.

"*Guten Morgen, Frau* Jordan and *kleiner* Peter," he said, putting out his hand to shake with the child.

Papa chuckled. Then, reaching in his pocket, he handed a small purse to Daniel. "The list is inside. We need only a few items — Manila rope, a sack of sugar, flour, salt, and coffee."

Daniel put the purse in his pocket. "I will get everything just as you want, *Herr* Jordan." Glancing at Mina he added, "So, it grows late."

They all walked down to the road, and Daniel climbed into the wagon.

In spite of Daniel's teasing about washday — or maybe because of it — Mina looked up at him with a saucy smile. "Are you sure you don't need somebody to protect you from the Indians?"

Grinning at her, he reached down and picked up his rifle. "I have my protector right here." Then his face grew serious. "Want to ride down the road a way with me, Mina?"

Mina turned to Papa.

"*Ja* sure, Mina, go ahead." He had that look of amusement that always came when Mina's spirit flared up.

Mina put one foot on a spoke and climbed into the wagon. Daniel cracked the whip over the oxen, and they started with a jolt.

"*Auf Wiedersehen*," Daniel called.

Peter began to cry, calling, "Mi — na," and reaching his arm out toward her while *Tante* held him back by the other.

Mina laughed. "Don't worry, Peter, I'm not going anywhere."

But Peter continued to cry for her.

The wagon creaked and swayed as the oxen plodded along the road. It was a fresh spring morning, the kind that should have made her joyful. But Mina hardly noticed the bluebonnets and Indian paintbrush that covered the meadow beside the road.

24

After riding in silence for a moment, Mina looked over at Daniel. "I dare you to take me along."

Daniel laughed. "I like your spirit, Mina."

"People always say that — you, Papa, Mister Allen. But a lot of good it does me. How much spirit does it take to wash clothes and sweep the cabin?" She paused. "I'd rather be captain of a ship or a Texas Ranger . . . "

Daniel looked at her. His eyes were full of merriment. "I think they do not take pretty girls with blonde braids." He tweaked one of her braids playfully and laughed.

"Stop it, Daniel." She stood up and jumped out of the wagon. "I'll show you . . . I'll cut them off!"

Daniel looked alarmed and stopped the oxen.

Mina started back along the road.

"Wait, Mina!"

She kept on. In a moment she heard the wagon start up again. It was a miserable way to say goodbye. She wanted to have one last glance and see if he was looking. But she did not allow herself to turn around. She hated Daniel for mocking her.

As Mina walked up the rise toward the washing tree, Papa stood up from his work and motioned for her to come to him. He probably knew what she was thinking.

"You know, Papa," she said when she stood before him, "sometimes I think I should have been born a boy so I could do what I want."

Papa looked at her quietly for a moment with his sad eyes.

"I'm glad you were born a girl, Mina. A girl with spirit." He paused. "Some would say I did wrong by teaching you to fire a shotgun, letting you run wild on Tucan."

"What do you say, Papa?"

"I say, I did not want to put out the fire, Mina. I still believe I was right. But now you are a young woman, and you must use your spirit in other ways."

"How, Papa? I cannot be like *Tante* or Anna. I would burst."

"No, I can see that. But there is more than one way to be a woman."

"But there aren't enough ways," Mina said. "Maybe I have the same yearnings as you did when you decided to leave Germany and come to Texas."

Papa thought about that for a moment. Then he said, "Germany had no need for me, and Texas did. And Texas needs strong women of spirit like you will be one day."

Mina looked over at the washing tree where *Tante* stirred the clothes in the big black pot. It was time for Mina to rinse and hang them out on the fence. For the life of her, she could not see but one way of being a woman.

5

News from
Fredericksburg

It would be over a week until she saw Daniel again, and the time passed slowly. On Monday Mina and *Tante* planted sweet potato slips in the morning. Wednesday from dawn to dusk they boiled lye and grease in the washpot until it turned into soft, jellylike soap. As Mina stirred with a long stick she thought of Daniel. She imagined him urging the oxen along toward home, cracking the whip over their heads.

On Saturday night Daniel had not returned. What could have happened? Mina wondered as she bathed in the wooden tub set near the hearth. Did an axle break or a wheel come loose? She tried to keep thoughts of Comanches away, but sometimes they came against her will. What if Comanches waylaid him? One rifle could not protect him from a raiding party. By the time he reloaded they could fire many arrows, and one might find its mark. She imagined that Daniel had fallen from the wagon, an arrow in his shoulder. The Comanches were throwing everything out of the wagon. Sacks of flour burst and covered the ground with white dust . . .

"Mina, are you nearly through with your bath?" *Tante* Lisette asked from the other side of the folding screen.

Grateful for her words that dispelled the vision, Mina picked up the yellow soap and rubbed it on the washcloth. "Almost." The fire sizzled and the clock ticked as Mina scrubbed herself and tried to think of less drastic reasons. But when none came to mind, she said, "Papa, I was just wondering why Daniel has not come home yet."

"Perhaps he decided to stop at Chief Custaleta's village," Papa suggested.

Mina seized upon that idea. *Ja*, there he was in Custaleta's tepee, lounging on a buffalo robe with the Chief and several young warriors. They passed the pipe around, and each one took a long, slow draw. The firelight flickered on Daniel's face.

Mina reached for the towel and stepped out of the tub, drying herself quickly. She slipped the night dress over her head and came around the screen.

Papa puffed on his pipe while *Tante* knitted some little socks for Peter. Mina sat down on the rug before the fire and warmed herself.

"Daniel can take care of himself, Mina," Papa said. "Any number of things could have happened. I remember once on a trip to Victoria when Peach Creek was up so high I had to camp there several days and wait for the waters to subside."

"*Ja*," *Tante* said, "and I worried myself nearly sick."

It was the sitting home, waiting and wondering, that Mina could not abide. If she could do as she pleased, she would jump on Tucan and ride away until she met up with Daniel.

Before going to bed that night, Mina pushed open the shutter window and looked out. The stars shone brightly in the cool spring night.

"Schnurri? Are you there?"

In a moment Schnurri came, and Mina sat down to write in her journal.

Saturday, April 29, 1850

Here I sit in my loft wondering where Daniel is tonight. Is he looking at the stars too? I wish I had not behaved so foolishly when he left. From now on I must strive to think before acting.

She closed the book, knelt beside her bed, and spoke a silent prayer:

Father, please watch over Daniel this night and bring him safely home tomorrow. If You will, I promise never to be rude or thoughtless again. Amen.

The cornshuck mattress rustled as she lay down in bed and settled into a comfortable position on her side. She lay a long time looking at the stars in the little square of sky through the window.

In the morning there was so much to do in preparation for going to church that Mina had no time to worry about Daniel. Once a month the circuit preacher came to Willow Creek, stayed with one of the families, and held service in the log schoolhouse. Mina liked these Sundays when Reverend Basse came. When the weather was good like today, everyone brought food and spread it out on a table under the giant liveoak after the church service was over. In the afternoon children might wade in the creek or climb trees, but no games were played on Sundays, just as no work was done. Sometimes the girls, big and little, went to a flowery place and wove wreaths of flowers to adorn their heads.

Mina straightened her bed, smoothed the blue coverlet, and climbed down the ladder.

Tante Lisette, who was pouring water in the coffee pot, said cheerily, "Perhaps Daniel will arrive while we are at church."

Mina smiled at her and hoped so. She went about her chores, stirring up the corn bread batter and frying the bacon while *Tante* packed their picnic dinner.

After breakfast Mina went up to her loft to dress. She pulled on black stockings and laced up her high-top shoes. Then she took her pale yellow muslin dress off the hook and slipped it over her head. She combed out her long, blonde hair and tied it back with a yellow satin ribbon.

Papa was out hitching the oxen. When the wagon was loaded, they climbed in. Papa and *Tante* Lisette sat on the spring seat while Mina sat on a board laid across the wagon box. She held Peter on her lap. He loved to ride in the wagon and name things they saw along the way — butterflies, a buzzard, grasshoppers. *Tante* tied on her bonnet, but Mina did not like wearing one. She wanted to feel the wind in her hair and the sun on her face.

At the schoolhouse, everyone parked near the tree, unhitched the oxen and horses, and greeted one another. Anna ran over to Mina, and the two girls hugged. Pretty and ladylike, Anna never looked mussed. Soft brown curls peeked out from her Sunday bonnet.

"Why do you suppose Daniel isn't back yet?" she asked.

"I don't know. Papa says any number of things could have happened. Maybe he stopped at Chief Custaleta's village."

Once again Mina was plunged into worry. He *should*

be back by now. What if he never came back? Mina glanced at *Frau* Hessler who, though in the midst of greeting friends, seemed isolated with concern for her son.

Mina and Anna took hands and walked away from the gathering to the bank overlooking Willow Creek.

Perhaps in an effort to cheer Mina, Anna said, "Remember the time you said you were going to ask Daniel to marry you?" She giggled at the thought.

Mina smiled, remembering how silly she had been. "*Ja,* but now I've changed my mind."

"But everyone knows you two are sweet on each other."

"I know, Anna. Truly I do like Daniel. It's just that there are so many things I want to do."

"Like what?"

Mina hesitated. How could she tell Anna she wanted to be a ship's captain or a Texas Ranger?

"You just don't want to grow up, Mina!"

Maybe what Anna said was true. Mina did not know for sure.

"Sometimes I do and sometimes I don't, Anna. Don't you ever yearn for something more?"

"What do you mean?"

"Don't you ever wish you could go places and do things?"

Anna shook her head. "Crossing the Atlantic Ocean was enough for me."

"But, just think, Anna, when you have babies, that is the end of your life!"

"No, it is not! It's the *beginning.* I *want* to get married and have babies. If only I could find someone."

Anna did not understand her either, so Mina quit trying. Instead she asked, "What about *Herr* Lange? Do you still fancy him?"

31

Anna blushed prettily and nodded yes. *Herr* Lange was the schoolmaster. He had left for a few weeks of vacation during spring planting.

Elizabeth Dannheim, who was fourteen, came to join them just in time to see Anna blush in answer to Mina's question.

"Oh, tell what made you blush, Anna, please do. I want to know."

Anna shook her head, smiling sweetly.

Just then someone rang the school bell. It was time to go in for the service. Mina hurriedly tied on her bonnet and started toward the schoolhouse. The three girls were the last ones to enter, and they sat on a bench in the back on the women's side.

Reverend Basse, a big weathered man with kindly eyes, stood at the front of the room. "We begin our divine service in the name of the Father, the Son, and the Holy Spirit. Let us sing 'My Shepherd the Lord.' "

Herr von Trappe stood up then with his violin and began to play as everyone sang:

> *My shepherd the Lord*
> *Of this I'm so glad . . .*

Mina sang out with vigor, as did everyone. Singing brought them together in a way that made something well up inside Mina, and often tears came to her eyes. *Herr* von Trappe was also caught up in the rapture of the music, and his whole body swayed as he drew the bow across the strings.

After the hymn Reverend Basse said a prayer in his deep, booming voice. He asked God to watch over Daniel during his journey home. Surely, Mina thought, God would hear and answer his prayer. No one could ignore such a voice.

Even when Reverend Basse said things Mina could not understand, she loved the power of his voice and his careful articulation of each word. In the sermon he urged them to forget their cares and think on eternal joy.

Mina tried, but she was not sure exactly what eternal joy was. She *did* know what eternal waiting was, however.

When the service was over, Reverend Basse stood at the door, shaking hands and talking as people left the schoolhouse and moved toward the spreading liveoak. The women and girls began to bring bowls and platters of food to the heavy puncheon table. Mina climbed into the wagon and handed *Tante* the bowl of sauerkraut. Standing there for a moment, she glanced southward and saw dust rising beyond the nearest hill.

"It's Daniel," she exclaimed, flinging off her bonnet and jumping down from the wagon. She heard his name repeated among the crowd, but she did not stop to talk. She ran along the wagon track road until she rounded a curve and there he was, his hair the color of sunshine. Mina waved as she ran, and Daniel waved back, shouting "whoa" at the oxen.

She stopped at the wagon, panting for breath. Daniel's face looked weary, as though he had not slept all night.

"I was afraid . . . something had happened," she said between breaths.

"It did."

"What?" Mina thought it could not have been too bad, because here he was, alive.

"Climb in. I'll tell you as we ride."

When she had sat down on the spring seat beside him, he said, "You look very pretty."

Mina looked straight ahead. "Thank you, Daniel."

33

She did not know what else to say, and yet his eyes stayed on her.

"Well, what *did* happen?"

"It was the Comanches. They stole some horses from the Schuesslers' place near Fredericksburg, and when Wilhelm Schuessler saw them, he ran to sound the alarm. The Comanches overtook him, killed him, and carried away his little son, Max.

Mina covered her mouth with her hands. She knew them, except for the boy.

"The neighbors gave chase to save the boy," Daniel went on, "but the Comanches got away. *Herr* Guenther and a group have gone to Austin to ask Governor Bell to call up the Texas Rangers. We are going to chase those savages back to *Comanchería* for good."

"We?"

"*Ja,* I am joining up, Mina. I sent a letter to the governor volunteering my services."

6

Visitors

One morning when April had turned into May, Mina was in the garden hoeing weeds when she heard the clomping of horses' hoofs. Dropping the hoe, she hiked up her skirts, climbed the fence, and ran barefoot through the orchard out to the road. A group of horsemen came riding along, and at their head was a lean, broad-shouldered man who slouched in the saddle. It was her old friend, William Allen.

"Mister Allen!" Mina called, running down the road to meet him.

A smile creased his cheeks as he reined in his prancing horse, Yack.

"Can this be the same Mina — all grown up?" he asked when she stood breathless beside his horse.

"The same." Mina looked around at the group of ten or twelve men. Two of them were Lipan Apaches. "You

35

wouldn't be the company of Rangers that Governor Bell called up, would you?"

"The same, *Fräulein*. You can call me *Captain* Allen now."

"Truly? A Ranger captain?"

"Yep," he said, chuckling at her amazement. "And this is Lieutenant Burleson, my second in command." He indicated the man who rode at his side.

The lieutenant took off his hat revealing curly red hair. "I'm pleased to meet you, Miss Jordan," he said in a quiet voice.

With a wave of his arm, Captain Allen said, "And these are the men who will chase the Comanches out of Texas — some of them anyway."

Mina nodded to the Rangers. Never had there been so many visitors to Willow Creek. She bounced up on her toes with excitement. "You *are* staying for dinner, aren't you?"

"Is that an invitation?"

"Yes . . . now come up to the cabin. Papa and *Tante* Lisette will be so pleased to see you."

Mina flung her braids behind her shoulders and started along the road, walking beside William Allen.

"How's that Comanche horse of yours?" he asked.

"Still a little wild, but I like him that way."

He laughed. "Yep, I guess he'll always be a mustang at heart."

William Allen had gotten Tucan in trade with a Comanche for some glass beads. He gave the horse to Mina one Christmas when he passed through and stayed with the Jordans. The name Tucan meant "night" in Comanche language, and he *was* black as night with one white forefoot and two slit ears, a Comanche mark.

Papa stood watching them from where the road turned up to the cabin. "William! I should have guessed you would be leading the Rangers. The governor could not have chosen more wisely."

"Thank you, Ernst."

The men all dismounted and stood about, waiting.

Tante Lisette came out of the door leading Peter by the hand.

"Who is that young man you have there, *Frau* Jordan?" Allen said.

Peter hid his face in her skirts, and the men chuckled.

"It has been too long since you paid us a visit, William," *Tante* said.

"Well, I think this crowd will more than make up for it," Allen replied.

"You are welcome, William. We'll add some potatoes to the *Kartoffelsalat* and make enough for all."

"Thank you, *Frau* Jordan."

"Mina, you run and fetch water," *Tante* said, "and Ernst, we'll need some sausage." Then taking Peter by the hand, she led him up to the cabin as he looked back at the Rangers.

While the men were taking care of their horses, Papa and Captain Allen brought sausage from the smokehouse. Then they sat at the table sipping coffee as Mina and *Tante* peeled potatoes and listened to them talk. Peter played on the rug with some wooden blocks.

Papa shook his head sadly. "It's too bad the Comanches don't abide by Meusebach's treaty."

"A treaty means nothing to those savages, Ernst. They kill and take what they want, regardless of whether it's from a Texan or a German . . . or even another tribe."

He paused a moment. "I must tell you some more bad news."

Mina stopped and looked at him, waiting.

"When we came by Custaleta's to recruit the Lipan guides, we learned that the same band of Comanches rode near their village on the way north. The Chief's daughter was out gathering berries alone, and they kidnapped her too."

"Amaya?" Mina suddenly stood up, and the potatoes rolled out of her lap onto the floor and under the table.

Allen nodded and began to help *Tante* Lisette pick them up while Mina stood still, trying to understand. Then he went on. "When Custaleta discovered she was missing he set out to follow with his best warriors, but it was too late. They had escaped with her. And the Chief was wounded by one of the Comanches who doubled back."

Mina sat down. "How bad?"

"He'll recover from the wound, but not from the loss of Amaya. She was his favorite daughter."

Papa shook his head. "I know how he must feel."

"What will they do to her?" Mina asked Captain Allen.

"Well, she'll probably be handed over to an old squaw at first. Then, if she behaves, one of the young warriors might take her for his wife."

Amaya would never want to marry a Comanche. She had told Mina once that Comanche women were mere slaves to their men and grew old while still young.

"And what if she does not behave?"

William Allen looked at her with pain in his deep-set eyes. "I'd rather not speculate on that, *Fräulein*. Look, I know she is your friend, and we'll do our best to bring her back. And the boy too."

"Can I go?" Mina blurted.

Papa and Allen chuckled, and Mina felt herself blush. At times, it seemed, she heard words coming from her mouth even before thinking them. What did the verse from Proverbs say? *Whoso keepeth his mouth and his tongue keepeth his soul from troubles.* The words of wise King Solomon. She wondered if *he* ever had feelings that had to get out. But he was king and could do as he pleased, while she was a girl and must do as others wished. More than anything she wished to go with Captain Allen and rescue Amaya from the savages. Instead she went on peeling potatoes in silence.

Allen was showing his new pistol to Papa.

"The governor presented me with a pair of these big beauties. It's a Walker Colt — easy to load, shoots six times."

Papa examined the pistol. "If every man had one of these, there would be no more Comanche trouble."

Allen watched thoughtfully as Papa turned the pistol from side to side. Then standing, he pulled his old five-shooter from his belt and handed it to Papa.

"Ernst, why don't you have my old revolver?"

"*Nein,* William, some of your men may need it."

"They have their own weapons. Besides," he looked at Mina, "I think this young lady has always wanted to learn how to shoot it." His eyes crinkled almost shut when he smiled.

Mina glanced at Papa. It was true. She *had* admired that revolver with its polished walnut grip and finely engraved cylinder. But learning to shoot it was not exactly ladylike.

Papa hesitated, frowning, his wide mouth turned down at the corners.

"Oh, Papa, do please take it."

William Allen laughed heartily. "What did I tell you? Now, take it, Ernst, with my thanks for your hospitality."

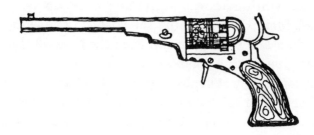

"Very well, William," Papa said at last. "Thank you kindly."

"Good. Here, let me show you how to load," Allen said. "It requires a little patience. You have to take the gun apart." He tapped out a wedge and removed the barrel and cylinder. Then he opened his possibles bag and took out the powder flask, balls, and caps. Holding the cylinder in his palm, he poured powder into the empty chambers.

"First the powder, then the ball," he said, looking at Mina.

She nodded. She knew that, of course, from loading Papa's shotgun, but it was a good idea to repeat the saying.

Allen placed a lead ball on each chamber, forcing it in with a ball seat. He put the revolver back together again and inserted the percussion caps. "Now she's ready to fire."

"I feel more secure already," *Tante* Lisette said, putting some sausage in the Dutch oven and placing it over the coals.

"You are more secure, *Frau* Jordan. Chief Custaleta tells me there is not a Comanche anywhere around here — they have all ridden back to *Comanchería*. And we plan to chase them still farther."

Allen stood up then and said, "I need to ride over to the Hesslers' before dinner. I understand Daniel wants to join our company."

"Fine, William," Papa said.

As Captain Allen started out the door he turned and looked at Mina. She was dumping potatoes into a pot of boiling water.

"Tell you what, *Fräulein,* after dinner I'll give you a quick shooting lesson. How's that?"

"Oh, William, I don't think she should," *Tante* Lisette began.

"Leave her be this time, Lisette. It will do no harm," Papa said.

Mina looked at Papa, surprised. He had that sparkle in his eyes. Turning to Allen she said, "I'd like that, Mister . . . *Captain* Allen."

7

A Plan

As Mina and *Tante* Lisette busied themselves preparing dinner for the Rangers, Anna appeared at the open door.

"Guten Morgen, Frau Jordan, Mina." Her face was alight with excitement. "I *had* to come over and find out what is happening." She took off her sunbonnet and sat down on the bench beside the table.

Mina was emptying cottage cheese from a cloth bag into a bowl. "It's William Allen," she said. "He's captain of the company of Texas Rangers you saw out there."

" I *thought* they were Rangers."

Mina wrung the bag over the bowl of cheese to get the last drops. Then, walking to the door, she said, "Come, Anna, I need to wash this out." She paused on the threshold, watching *Tante* Lisette spread the embroidered linen cloth over the table. It gave a touch of ele-

42

gance to the cabin. "Shall we pick some flowers for the table, *Tante?*"

"*Ja,* that would be nice, Mina."

From the washstand they could see the group of Rangers and two Lipans standing about down by the well. Papa was with them, holding Peter by the hand.

"Who are those two Indians?" Anna asked.

"Guides from Custaleta's village." Mina dipped water into the basin. "Guess what news Captain Allen brought."

"What?"

"The Comanches kidnapped Amaya."

"Oh, Mina, how awful." A frown creased Anna's smooth, pale forehead.

"I asked Captain Allen if I could go with them to look for her, but he only laughed," Mina said, hanging the bag on the towel peg to dry.

"Did you think he would let you?"

"I didn't think, I just asked. But he's going to teach me to shoot the revolver he gave Papa."

"Maybe you should have been a boy, Mina — then you could run off and join the Rangers like Daniel." Anna giggled at the thought.

"Maybe." Mina did not laugh, even though Anna had been joking. She held the thought in her mind as they picked bluebonnets and brought them back to the cabin.

Tante was looking at the table, hands on her hips. "Well, all is ready. Won't you have dinner with us, Anna?"

"Thank you, *Frau* Jordan, but I must go home. Mama will be waiting to hear the news."

When Anna had left, Mina put the flowers in a jar and set it on the table. Then she went out on the porch to ring the dinner bell.

43

Papa, Peter, and Captain Allen led the way to the cabin. The men, washed and combed, bowed their heads as Papa spoke a blessing in German.

The Rangers, who had brought their own tin plates and utensils, entered the cabin talking and laughing, eager for the good, home-cooked meal. They filed by, politely thanking *Frau* Jordan for her hospitality as they piled their plates with sausage, potato salad, and cottage cheese. They were all young men. One sandy-haired, freckled youth who looked to be about Daniel's age said his name was Ira Crenshaw.

Mina fixed a plate for Peter and lifted him into his high chair so he could watch. He sat eating thin slices of sausage with his fingers. When the two Lipans came to the table, he forgot about eating. One was a big, friendly fellow, but Peter's eyes were on the other — a small, fierce-looking warrior with red paint across his cheeks and eyelids.

Seeing them so close and inside the cabin, Peter began to cry and reached out to Mina. She picked him up saying, "They are *good* Indians, Peter." Peter was not convinced and clung to her until the Lipans had gone outside to eat.

"You funny little boy," Mina chided, putting him back in his high chair.

After supper the Rangers crowded around a steaming pan of soapy water and washed their own dishes. When the cleanup was finished, Captain Allen and Mina walked out past the Indian tree to the hill west of the cabin to have her shooting lesson. Now, more than ever, Mina wanted to learn to fire the revolver. An idea had come to her — an idea that was growing into a plan. And for that plan to work, she must be able to handle the revolver like a man.

"How about that white rock sticking up beside the tree as a target?"

"All right." Mina pulled back the hammer with her thumb and sighted down the barrel, squinting her left eye.

"Steady now, squeeze slowly on the trigger."

Her arm wavered, and she put her left hand up to steady it. When the rock was in the sight she pulled the trigger.

BLAM!

The shot went above the rock and hit the hillside beyond.

"You jerked up, *Fräulein*. Remember, don't *pull* the trigger. *Squeeze*. Now try it again."

Mina cocked the revolver, took aim carefully, and again steadied her arm.

"When you're ready, squeeze gently . . . gently."

BLAM! A piece flew off the rock where she nicked the left side.

"That's right, *Fräulein*. You've got the idea. All you need is practice."

Full of her success, Mina said, "Would you let a girl go with you if she could shoot like a man?"

He threw back his head and laughed.

Mina said nothing. She did not like his always laughing at her.

"No, I'm afraid not, Mina." He was still chuckling, shaking his head back and forth.

"But Amaya is out there . . . and I want to do something."

Allen's expression sobered. His eyes lost their merriment as he looked directly at her. "You're a young woman now. It wouldn't be proper."

Mina felt anger rising inside her, and the words burst out of her mouth. "I don't *care* about being proper."

Captain Allen swallowed, his Adam's apple rising and falling.

"Sure you do. Why, one of these days some young man will come along and . . ."

Mina did not want to hear the rest of her future as predicted by William Allen. She handed the revolver back to him, turned, and ran to the porch where she took Tucan's bridle from the peg.

Her horse was grazing near the well, and he lifted his head as she approached.

"Let's go for a ride, Tucan."

He let her slip the bit into his mouth and the bridle over his slit black ears. As soon as she unhobbled him, Tucan began to prance. Mina gave a leap onto his back and headed him out to the road. He broke into a gallop without any urging.

A confusion of thoughts crowded her mind. She could ride and shoot as well as a man, if not better. Why shouldn't she be allowed to go with them? It was *her* friend who had been kidnapped. Why must she stay here and wait? Well, maybe she wouldn't.

As Tucan galloped along, the wind washed over Mina, calming her, and she began to think clearly. First, she would cut her hair and dress like a boy. Didn't *Tante* have some of her brother's outgrown clothing in a trunk? Then — her heart leaped at the next part of the plan — tonight after everyone was asleep, she would ride to Custaleta's village, get a guide, and follow Captain Allen.

By the time Mina returned to the cabin the Rangers were mounting up. She did not want Captain Allen to leave until she had a chance to apologize for being rude. In her prayer she had promised God *never* to be rude again, but it seemed *never* was a word she should *never* use.

Tying Tucan to the garden fence rail, Mina started

over to Allen. Daniel stepped out of the group of Rangers into her path and caught her by the shoulders.

"Whoa, slow down a minute, Mina."

"I have to tell Captain Allen something," she said, struggling to get away.

"You have to tell me goodbye first." His strong hands held her securely in place.

She looked up at him, at his blue eyes that were amused at her and at his blond hair that always fell slanting across his forehead.

"I don't want to tell you goodbye. I want to go with you."

This time he did not laugh. His eyes grew serious. "I know you are worried about Amaya, but a company of Rangers is no place for a girl."

Mina wrested herself from his hands. She wanted to say, *Then where is the place for a girl — waiting at home? No thanks, Daniel Hessler. I'm coming along, like it or not.*

But, for once, she held back, swallowing hard to get the words down. "You are right, Daniel, it's no place for a girl," she said and in her mind added, *unless she is disguised as a boy.*

Daniel looked at her closely as if wondering whether to believe what he heard. She raised her chin, defying him not to.

"Well, then, *auf Wiedersehen,*" Daniel said. He paused, looking down at his boots and then back up at her boldly. "Will you think of me while I'm away?"

She grinned at him. "I'll try, Daniel Hessler, I'll try real hard."

He took a playful swipe at her chin with his fist, and she turned and ran over to Captain Allen.

"Well, *Fräulein,* you've become quite a rider. You stick to that horse like a Comanche."

47

"That's what *Tante* says too. Like a wild Indian."
Mina smiled at him, glad he was not angry with her.
"Anyway, I'm sorry for running off like that, but many
thanks for the lesson."

"It was just youthful high spirits, *Fräulein*." Then,
looking at her intently, he said, "I promise to do everything possible to bring back the Chief's daughter. Chaa
and Batsosé will see to that." He nodded toward the two
Lipan guides mounted on their horses with the Rangers.
"Well, we must be off." He mounted Yack, who tossed his
head upward to loosen the reins. "Thanks for your hospitality, and *auf Wiedersehen.*"

"*Auf Wiedersehen,* goodbye," they all called, and
Peter waved his short, plump arms. Mina looked quickly
at Daniel, waving to him as he turned his chestnut horse,
Red Dancer, and followed Captain Allen down the road,
beyond the cornfield, and out of sight.

8

Secret Preparations

That evening when *Tante* Lisette went out to milk, taking Peter with her, Mina was left to set supper on the table. But first she wrapped some corn bread and sausage in a cloth and tied it up.

Then she went in *Tante's* room and opened the trunk. Digging underneath the mending, Mina found a pair of brown denim trousers, a blue-striped shirt, and a woolen jacket that had belonged to *Tante's* brother. There was a button missing on the jacket, but she could fix that. She might need to adjust the waist of the trousers too.

On a table beside the bed sat a tin box with needles, thread, scissors, and buttons. Mina took out what she needed. Glancing around the room, she spied an old floppy hat of Papa's. Hurriedly she grabbed it off the peg, climbed the ladder to her loft, and hid everything under the bed.

After supper and the Bible reading, they all bowed their heads while Papa prayed.

Our Heavenly Father, watch over our loved ones, Daniel and William, as they go forth. Grant that they may find Amaya and the boy and bring them safely home.   Amen.

Mina said her own silent prayer. *And please, God, add Mina to that. I promise never . . . I promise to try to hold my tongue.*

As *Tante* Lisette washed the dishes, Mina wiped them. Her mind was on the night ahead and what she must do to carry out the plan. Was she brave enough to go out in the night alone? Captain Allen had said there were no more Comanches in these parts. But what else was out there? A panther? Tucan could outrun a panther.

Mina picked up a plate from the rinse pan, and it slipped out of her fingers to the floor, shattering.

Peter came running to her. "Uh-oh, Mina break," he said, pointing to the pieces on the floor.

"Oh, be quiet, Peter," Mina said.

Peter looked at her a moment, his mouth turned down. Then he ran to his mother, hugged her around the knees, and began to cry.

"Mina, how could you? Look how you've upset him."

Mina said nothing as she stooped down to pick up the pieces.

"Is something bothering you?" Papa asked her.

"No, nothing," Mina said hastily. She must be more careful or Papa might suspect something. She stretched out her arms to Peter. "Come, Peter, I'm sorry."

He ran to her arms, and everything was all right again.

There was much left to be done, and Mina said good night to Peter, *Tante* Lisette, and Papa, giving them each a kiss on the cheek.

"Going to bed so early, Mina?" Papa asked.

"*Ja,* I want to read some in the Bible." She hoped God would forgive her for that lie.

"That is good." He put his arms around her. "I don't know what I would do without you, *kleine* Mina." He patted her on the back.

She clung to him for a moment as her throat tightened. "Or I without you, Papa." Her voice sounded choked. She had to get away or lose her resolve.

Picking up the Bible and a candle, she made her way slowly up the ladder.

First she would write a note to Papa and then do the mending. When everyone was in bed, she would cut her hair.

Mina unlatched the shutter and pushed it open. Rising above the treetops, a full moon lighted the earth like a cold, mystical sun. It glinted on the rivulet of water in Willow Creek and shone on Anna's cabin on the other side.

Schnurri was waiting, meowing on the roof. Mina reached up and lifted her in. Then, sitting down at her desk, she tore out a blank page of her journal. The candle flame guttered as a soft breath of air entered the open window. Mina moved the candle to one side and began to write:

Dear Papa,

I have gone to Chief Custaleta's village for a guide because I want to follow Captain Allen and rescue Amaya.

If you love me, let me go.

Your loving
kleine Mina

That done, she took out the jacket and began to sew on a button. Downstairs *Tante* put Peter in his bed in the corner, and Papa played the harmonica softly to lull him to sleep. It was a sweet, sad melody that made her throat ache.

Listening to Papa's harmonica was Mina's favorite way to fall asleep. On nights when he returned from his

51

hauling trips, he always played before going to bed. It was as if he brought back the long, slow days of riding across country in the wagon, and turned them into music. Mina would lie on her bed in the loft, safe once again with Papa in the cabin, and give herself up to sleep as he played.

Even now she felt tempted to blow out the candle, crawl into bed, and let Papa's music carry her off to sleep.

But when he stopped playing, the spell was broken. She heard the scraping as Papa shoveled ashes onto the hot coals. That meant they were going to bed. Mina went back to work, sticking her finger once with the needle as she searched for the hole in the button.

When the door closed to their sleeping room and all was quiet, she stripped down to her vest and drawers and pulled on the trousers for fit. The waist was a little loose, so she moved the button over. It must fit tightly enough to hold the revolver.

Then it was time to cut her hair. She stepped quietly across the floor, looked in the mirror on the table, and took hold of her right braid.

Mina hesitated for a moment, remembering another time she had cut her hair. It was when she first met Chief Custaleta and he asked for locks of her hair. She had cut off her braids just above the ribbons with a sharpened piece of bone.

She set the scissors to the braid. Her hair was thick, and she had to cut and cut to get through.

There, it was done. Holding the severed braid in her hand, she stared at it as if she did not fully comprehend. Suddenly she brightened. Of course, I'll give them to Custaleta. She caught hold of the other and cut through it also.

The face that looked back at her from the mirror frowned. Her stubby hair hung unevenly around her ears. Now she *had* to go, for she could never face *Tante* in the morning like this. She snipped at the longer hair to even it up. Better to be a trim boy than an untidy one.

When Mina had finished dressing, she put the braids in her pocket. On a peg hung the fringed doeskin dress and leggings Wapako had given her. Without knowing why, she rolled them up in a blanket along with her moccasins, beaded belt, her slicker, and the bag of food.

Then she blew out the candle. Moonlight shone in through the window onto the blue coverlet. On the table sat Johanna. Her painted china face glowed and her bright red mouth smiled as though she approved of what Mina was about to do. She always gave Mina a feeling that everything was right with the world. For just an instant she thought of carrying her along in the bedroll too. But she quickly dismissed the idea. One did not go to join up with the Rangers carrying a doll!

Schnurri roused herself from her pillow under the eave, aware that her mistress was not settling into bed as usual. She came meowing and rubbing against her trouser leg. Holding Schnurri and the bedroll under her arm and her shoes in her hand, Mina climbed down the ladder.

She lifted the latch slowly and opened the front door. Schnurri leaped from atop the bedroll and ran off toward the garden. Outside, everything was visible — the garden fence, the corncrib, the orchard, Tucan standing in the moon shadow of the Indian tree. There was no reason to be afraid, Mina told herself. She knew the way to Custaleta's village by heart.

There was only one more thing — the revolver. She tiptoed to the fireplace, took it from the mantel, and stuck it in her belt. Over her shoulder she put the possibles bag containing the balls, caps, and powder flask.

Holding the latchstring, Mina shut the door, let the latch down, and stuffed the string back through the hole. Now she was locked out, and her heart lurched at the thought.

She took the bridle from its peg and walked toward Tucan. A rustling sound from near the fence startled her, and she stopped, catching her breath. Another rustle, and Schnurri leaped after something scurrying across the garden.

"Oh, it's only you, Schnurri. How silly of me to be afraid."

As she slipped the bridle on Tucan, he jerked his head up as though this was no time to go galloping across the countryside.

"Easy, Tucan," Mina said in a soothing voice. "I know you think your mistress has lost her wits."

In the shed at the back of the cabin she lifted the saddle from its peg without a sound, picked up the blanket, and lugged them back to where Tucan stood hobbled.

When he was saddled with the bedroll tied on behind, Mina led him down to the road, still carrying her shoes. There was movement in the grass along the creek bank. A raccoon family, a mother and three babies, waddled along with heads down, backs humped up. With Tucan at her side, Mina began to feel that she was not alone in the night. Other creatures went about their business unafraid, and she would too.

Sitting down beside the corncrib she put on her high-topped shoes and tied each bow with a determined tug. Then she stepped in the stirrup, and Tucan started off down the moonlit road.

9

Good Medicine

At Hedwig's Hill Mina turned off the road and headed toward Custaleta's village. She rode along the river until she came in sight of the silent array of tepees in the moonlight.

Her arrival in the middle of the night would be startling to the Lipans, so she decided to stop and call out to them.

She called once. "Chief Custaleta, it is Mi — na."

Immediately the dogs began to bark, first one and then the whole pack. She called again, but her voice was lost in the noise of the barking.

There was shadowy movement among the tepees. What if they don't recognize me? Mina thought. She reached in her pocket and took out the braids.

A horse whinnied, and in a moment a group of mounted warriors rode out of the village toward her.

Each carried a shield and lance. The blades flashed in the moonlight.

"Mi — na," she called desperately, but they could hear nothing over the pounding hoofs. She jerked the hat from her head and shook out her hair. Tucan backed up a few steps.

The Lipans surrounded her, their lances poised. One of them came close and reached toward her. Mina's heart leaped up. He grabbed the revolver from her belt, pointed it at her, and pulled back the hammer.

"No! Wait." Her pulse pounded in her ears. She must make him understand. "Mi — na," she said slowly and distinctly, and then in Spanish, "Girl-With-Hair-Like-Sun." She was breathless.

The warrior glowered at her a moment and then lowered the revolver. They spoke among themselves in Lipan words.

Mina grew bolder. She put the braids up to her head as if still attached.

"I Mi — na."

There was a pause.

Then the warrior who had the revolver threw back his head and laughed. They all laughed except one who sat his pinto horse tall and straight, studying her.

Mina looked at him. Could he be Chief Custaleta's elder son?

"Nakona?"

The laughter stopped.

He nodded to her. "*Sí*, Nakona. Why you come?" he asked in Spanish.

"I want to find Amaya. Need help of Chief Custaleta."

He said nothing. His face showed no expression.

Mina held out the braids to him. She knew the Lipans prized her blonde hair highly. "Give to your father. Maybe good luck."

Nakona took the braids and held them in his open palm. They shone silver in the moonlight. All was quiet except when a horse shook his reins and snorted.

Then Nakona held the braids on high, letting them dangle. Turning to the other warriors, he said, *"Iszeh inzoh!"*

Mina did not know what his words meant, but Nakona spoke to the warrior who had taken her revolver and motioned him to return it. He obeyed.

"You come to Chief's lodge, Girl-With-Hair-Like-Sun," Nakona said.

Mina nodded and, nudging Tucan with her heels, rode on to the village in the midst of the five warriors. She was safe now among Custaleta's people. If only he will agree to send a guide, she thought.

People had gathered at the edge of the village. As Nakona spoke to them, they made way. Upon reaching Custaleta's lodge, Nakona dismounted and called to his father, speaking Lipan words.

There was a single word of reply, and Nakona motioned for Mina to follow him into the tepee. One of the warriors took their horses. Inside was dark and smoky. A small fire in the center lighted the solemn faces of Custaleta and Wapako.

The Chief sat on his couch leaning on a backrest, his wounded leg covered with a blanket.

"You have come," he said in Spanish.

"Sí."

He motioned her to sit on the other side of the fire where a buffalo robe was spread. Wapako added some sticks of wood, and flames leaped up to embrace them.

After the period of silence, Wapako arose and brought

her a cup of water. "Drink," she said, and smiled sadly at Mina. Her long, dark hair hung loose down her back.

"I have sorrow that Amaya go away," Mina said. "She my blood sister."

Wapako nodded.

"I go with Rangers to find."

Nakona spoke in Lipan then, handing the braids to his father.

Wapako translated his words for Mina. "Nakona say you bring good medicine for save Amaya — you bring braids of hair-like-sun."

So that was what Nakona's words had meant when he said *iszeh inzoh* — good medicine.

"I bring gift for Chief Custaleta," Mina said. "If gift good medicine, then I have happiness." She looked into the expressionless face of the Chief. "Once you help my Papa when he have sickness. Now I want save Amaya from Comanches."

Chief Custaleta nodded. "How I can help my young friend?" he asked.

"Send warrior with me," Mina answered quickly.

There was a long silence as Custaleta pondered her request.

Then lifting his chin proudly, he said, "Nakona good son. I need . . . but send with you at first light." Custaleta gave Nakona one of the braids and spoke in Lipan to him.

Nakona nodded his willingness to go. He arose, bid good night, and left the tepee.

Wapako stood and spoke to Mina. "You sleep in my lodge." She motioned to a bed on the left side of the door.

It was not until Mina lay down at last on the buffalo robe that she realized how tired she was. She closed her eyes and sank into sleep immediately.

She had just closed her eyes, it seemed, when Wapako awakened her. The fire had been built up and Wapako was cooking ashcakes.

Mina arose and went out the circular doorway to the underbrush a short distance away. The sky was beginning to lighten, and birds twittered and sang from the post oak and mesquite trees. No one was about yet, so she walked down to the Llano River. She knelt on the grassy bank and washed her hands and face. It was going to be a sunny day, which gave her heart for the journey ahead. Had Papa discovered yet that she was gone? She wondered what he would do. Would he trust her?

When Mina returned to the tepee, Custaleta was sitting up, eating. Wapako handed her an ashcake.

"Eat. Shaman come soon."

The Shaman! Could it be the same Old One who had cured Papa long ago?

Mina ate hungrily.

In a few moments Nakona's voice called to Wapako from outside, and she bade him enter. The stooped Old One, supported by Nakona on one side and his cane on the other, made his way slowly to the fire. He was the same Shaman. His eyes were still black and keen — the only sign of vitality in his leathery face. If he recognized her, he did not show it.

He stopped beside the Chief and sat down. Nakona sat on the other side. Custaleta passed the pipe to the Shaman, who puffed smoke out in the four directions — first to the east, then south, west, and finally north. When he finished, Wapako knelt before the Shaman, dipped her finger in a bowl, and marked his forehead with yellow pollen. Then she offered him the braids.

He took them in his crooked fingers, dipped them in the pollen, and began to chant:

Hai, hai, godiyileh

He closed his eyes and waved the braids about.

Though most white men did not believe in Indian medicine, Mina did. She closed her eyes and listened to the Shaman's monotone chanting.

Then he stopped and seemed to lapse into sleep, his chin resting on his chest. Saliva drained from the corners of his mouth. In a moment he awoke, and Nakona helped him to his feet. The Shaman gave one braid to Chief Custaleta and the other to Nakona, and he walked out slowly on his old, bowed legs.

Mina looked at Wapako.

"You go now," Wapako said. "You safe with He-Who-Kill-Two-Buffalo-With-One-Arrow."

"*Muchas gracias,* Wapako."

Tears came to Wapako's eyes, and she embraced Mina.

Chief Custaleta stood in spite of his wound. He put his hand on Mina's shoulder. "The Shaman blesses your journey. Go now and return with my beloved daughter."

Mina nodded. "We return with Amaya, Chief Custaleta." She looked into his immobile face and saw the sadness in his eyes.

"*Godiyileh,* let there be strong medicine," the Chief said and nodded to her.

"*Godiyileh,*" Mina repeated as she stepped outside the door.

People had gathered around to watch. Nakona awaited her on his pinto with Tucan beside him. His quiver and shield hung over his left shoulder, and he carried a lance. Across his cheeks and the high ridge of his nose he had smeared a blaze of red paint. She took Tucan's reins and mounted, sitting as erect as the young warrior.

Nakona nodded to her. "It is time . . . *vamonos.*"

As they left the village Mina turned for one last wave. Then she gave Tucan a nudge with her heels, and the two of them galloped across the meadow, headed north.

10

Smoke on the Horizon

The route led along Comanche Creek. Mina and Nakona rode side by side, sometimes galloping the horses. It seemed that the whole world was hers to ride across on this early spring morning. The liveoaks were putting on new leaves, and the mesquite trees had covered themselves with feathery green foliage. With the cool wind brushing across her face, she felt that all things were possible. They would find Amaya and bring her home.

Where the creek branched off, Nakona slowed to a walk. "Now look for trail of Rangers," he said.

The ground was strewn with granite rubble. Grass and wildflowers and an occasional prickly pear grew amongst the rocks. Mina looked as they rode, but she was not sure what she was looking for.

Suddenly, Nakona stopped and pointed. "Trail of Rangers, see?"

"Where?"

Nakona dismounted and squatted on the ground. "You see rock kicked away here. Leave dark place on earth."

She got down from Tucan to have a closer look. She saw that the earth where the rock had been was darker and moist.

"And here," Nakona said, "grass crushed by hoof of horse. You see?"

Mina nodded. Such small signs. At first she could not see them without Nakona's help. As they rode on, she looked to both sides, pulling her hat down to shade her eyes from the sun which had risen high in a cloudless sky.

There! She saw a clump of Indian blankets flattened to the ground.

"Look, Nakona, is that a sign?"

He nodded.

Farther on she spotted a hoofprint where rocks had been dislodged.

"*Sí,*" Nakona said, "soon you learn to follow trail like Lipan. Girl-With-Hair-Like-Sun have eyes like hawk."

Mina laughed, but Nakona, like his father, rarely showed emotion — at least not to her. He saw everything, but his face revealed little of what he thought.

The sun burned hot on Mina's back. Her mouth and throat were dry. She longed for a drink of water, but the creek had curved away from their trail. If she wanted water she must drink from Nakona's water bag. Mina looked at it with distaste. The bag was made from a buffalo paunch. When Nakona noticed her looking at the bag, he offered her a drink.

As she brought the bag to her mouth, the thought of drinking from an animal's stomach made her gag, and she handed it back to Nakona. Holding it to his mouth, he tilted back his head and had a long drink.

64

Mina reached out her hand to have it again. This time she took water in her mouth. It tasted leathery but soothed her dry mouth and throat as it went down.

Nakona put it back on his belt. "You make good Lipan," he said.

Mina smiled. She liked his words. "I bring Lipan dress." She patted her bedroll. "Wapako give to me."

Nakona nodded once. "Maybe need sometime."

By noon their trail once again ran alongside Comanche Creek. Nakona motioned in that direction.

"We stop. Horses drink."

As they headed for water, Tucan picked up his gait. On the bank Mina dismounted, tied his reins loosely over the saddle horn, and stroked his black, silky mane. Tucan stepped into the creek and began to suck up the clear water where minnows darted about. She knelt, scooping up some water, drank, and splashed her face.

While Nakona filled his water bag, Mina stood and stretched. A breeze stirred the leaves of the liveoak branches overhead. She took off her hat and shook her hair loose. Looking at Papa's old floppy hat, she thought of him reading her note. Would he be angry? Or would he merely be saddened that his *kleine* Mina had gone away?

The horses drank their fill and moved away to crop the green grass growing along the bank. Mina got the food bag from Tucan's saddle and handed a piece of sausage to Nakona. He studied it curiously before tearing off a bite with his teeth. Then he nodded.

"Bueno," he said, and tore off another bite.

"You make good German," Mina said.

Nakona looked at her for a moment, then laughed, something Mina had never seen him do. Her mouth fell open.

He stopped laughing long enough to say, "You good Lipan. I good German. Very funny."

Mina laughed with him.

Then just as suddenly Nakona became himself again, his face immobile. He touched the medicine pouch tied at his waist where he kept Mina's blonde braid.

"You know what mean *godiyileh?*"

"*Sí*, it mean good medicine."

Nakona nodded. "It mean we find Amaya. We save."

Mina wanted to believe that. But first they must find the Rangers. And then Captain Allen would have to agree to her going along. She knew that her arrival would not be a complete surprise, but would he let her stay?

The sun was setting when they passed near the base of a hill. Nakona stopped. Pointing to the top he said, "We ride up, look to Rangers."

Mina followed him along a zig-zag route up the slope. They went slowly, for the horses had to pick their way through crumbling limestone ledges and rocks.

At the top Mina dismounted. She felt short standing on the ground after riding Tucan all those hours. Her bottom was sore and her legs were rubbed raw. She walked stiffly to where Nakona stood on a ledge looking out to the north. Mina looked too, but all she could see was ridge after ridge of hills gradually fading into blue.

Then Nakona pointed. "Smoke . . . you look . . . by two hills."

In a gap between hills a thin plume of smoke arose, maybe ten miles away. Someone's campfire. Was it Rangers or Comanches?

"Comanches?" Mina asked.

Nakona shook his head. "Comanches no make fire." He walked to his horse. "We go now."

They rode toward the gap until darkness came on. At a creek crossing Nakona said, "We rest here. Wait for moon."

Mina was glad for the rest. Dismounting, she rubbed her bottom gingerly. Then she removed Tucan's bridle so he could graze without a bit in his mouth. He blew through his nostrils and shook his head.

After eating some jerky and ashcakes that Nakona offered her from his parfleche bag, Mina got her blanket. She wrapped it around her and sat down on the ground beneath a liveoak. The night had turned cool and wind swept across the land, soughing in the branches. It was a vast, lonely sound.

She shivered, not only from the cold but from the dark emptiness of the place. This was Comanche country —*Comanchería*. By all rights she should not be here. Comanches did not like white man entering their territory. They could be out there in the dark right now, ready to attack and carry her off. She listened to the sounds around her, but there was only the wind. Listening did no good, though, because Comanches could approach without a sound.

Suddenly, she wanted to be back in the cozy, safe cabin, lying on her own bed, listening to the wind outside her loft window.

But what about Amaya? She was a prisoner in an enemy tribe's camp. How much more she must yearn to be back in the tepee of her mother.

Nakona sat silently, wrapped in a blanket and his own thoughts, smoking a sotol shuck cigarette.

"Nakona?"

He grunted.

She needed to talk, but it was difficult in Spanish. How could she tell him she was afraid?

Instead she asked, "Amaya have fear?"

Nakona did not reply for a moment. Mina could not see his face in the dark. She waited.

"Daughter of Chief no have fear." He paused. "Girl-With-Hair-Like-Sun no have fear."

Did he mean that she *didn't* have fear or that she *mustn't* have fear? Mina looked over at him. His cigarette glowed as he drew on it, lighting up the high, hooked bridge of his nose.

The fact was she *did* have fear on this lonely creek bank. Tears came to her eyes and spilled out, running down her cheeks. She wiped them on her sleeve.

Without turning to look at her, he said, "Nakona no let harm come to Girl. You sleep now. Nakona watch for moon."

At that moment Mina felt she just about loved this proud son of a chief. No matter that she was a German girl from across the ocean and he a fearless warrior, he understood what she was feeling and had comforted her. For that she was grateful. Those few words spoken in his monotone, expressionless voice had reassured her, renewed her dream of saving Amaya.

Mina lay down and let her eyes close. Nakona was not afraid here in the darkness. He seemed to be part of it, part of the bank and trees and wind. She must try to put away her fears and be more like him.

She had no sooner fallen asleep than someone was nudging her shoulder. Mina sat up with a start, her heart pounding.

"Moon up," Nakona said. Then he went about readying the horses, putting Tucan's bridle back on.

The lopsided moon was rising behind the treetops, once again lighting up the night. Mina stood up stiffly and stretched. Remembering her resolve to put away her fears, she went off to the bushes.

When she returned, Nakona said, "You ready go?" His silver breastplate glinted like armor in the moonlight.

"Sí." Mina rolled her blanket and tied it behind the saddle.

They rode in silence as the moon made its way across the sky. At the top of a rise Nakona raised his bow over his head to signal a halt. He pointed ahead to a dark line of trees that snaked along both sides of a river.

"Rangers camp there on San Saba River."

Mina's heartbeat quickened. What would Captain Allen say when he saw her? Would he send her home? And what would Daniel think?

"Take off hat. Show hair."

Mina did as Nakona said, and they approached the river slowly. While still a distance away she called, "Hel–lo . . . Captain Allen?"

No answer.

A little closer Mina saw the campfire in a grove of trees across the river.

"Captain Allen?"

"Who goes?" someone shouted from a ledge on the near side of the river.

It was Daniel's voice.

11

Alemán Sister

"Daniel, it's Mina."

He emerged from behind a bush growing on the ledge. His golden shock of hair shone in the moonlight. He carried a rifle.

"Mina?"

"*Ja,* it's me. I cut my hair."

"What are you doing here?"

"I told you I wanted to come along, remember?"

Daniel groaned. "Captain Allen will be angry."

"I don't care."

"He'll send you back for sure."

Mina looked at Nakona, who sat his horse proud and aloof beside her. "Daniel say Captain Allen send home."

Nakona turned to Daniel and spoke his words with assurance. "No send home."

"Who is he?" Daniel asked.

"Chief Custaleta's son."

"Captain Allen is in charge here, not the Lipans. And he's not going to let a girl stay with the Rangers."

"But I'm a boy, Daniel. Don't I look like one?"

Daniel turned and started back toward the river. "No," he flung over his shoulder.

He would get over his anger when the surprise wore off, she thought, but Captain Allen was another matter. She dreaded coming face to face with him.

They dismounted and followed Daniel down rocky ledges to the river. Shallow water flowed around huge slabs of limestone. Mina leaped from one to the next as she led Tucan across.

The camp was set up in a grove of trees close to the river. And near the edge stood a shadowy group of men watching them cross. A tall, slouching figure came forward to meet Daniel. It was Captain Allen. Lieutenant Burleson stepped up beside him. Mina held her breath. She heard Daniel say her name in a low voice. Allen straightened from his usual slouch, looking in her direction.

Before he could speak, the two Lipan guides came to the edge of the river and greeted Nakona. *"Nini, shikisen."*

Nakona stepped ashore, and they patted one another on the shoulders, speaking Lipan words.

"Come, Tucan." Mina took the last jump to shore holding Tucan's reins and stood face to face with Captain Allen.

Moonlight shone on his lean face, but his deep-set eyes were in shadow. Though the men around him talked among themselves, Captain Allen studied her silently for a moment, hands on hips. Then without warning he said, *"Fräulein,* what in thunder are you doing here?"

His words seemed to hit her in the face. She stepped back and one foot slipped into the water.

"Fräulein?" The word was murmured through the group of Rangers as they gathered around for a closer look.

Mina felt her blood rising. She stepped back on the shore firmly. "Yes, *Fräulein.* I'm a girl. Johanne Ernestine Wilhelmine Jordan. I've come to rescue my friend, Amaya, from the Comanches, and if you won't let me join you I'll go on alone." The words came without thought — desperate, angry words.

The men seemed momentarily stunned by the outburst. The only sound was the calling of tree frogs back and forth across the river.

Then the men began talking among themselves and laughing. But Captain Allen, the lieutenant, and Daniel did not laugh or even smile. Instead, Allen turned to Nakona and spoke in Spanish. "Why you bring her here?"

"Girl-With-Hair-Like-Sun good medicine." Nakona showed the golden braid. "Shaman say good medicine. My father, Chief Custaleta, say Nakona go with Girl."

To Mina, Captain Allen said, "Does your Papa know where you've run off to?"

Mina nodded. "I left a note."

"Do you realize you are risking your life . . . and your honor . . . by coming out here? The Comanches would like nothing better than a young blonde woman to take home as a bride. Would you like that?"

"No!" she shot back at the captain. "But they won't know I'm a girl in this disguise."

"Comanches have ways of finding out, Mina," Allen said grimly. "Anyway, what they do with boys is even worse. They're just animals."

"But I thought you would help me, that you were my friend."

"I am — and your Papa's too. That's the reason you

73

and Nakona will start back first thing in the morning. Ernst is probably on his way right now to find you." To Nakona he said in Spanish, "Tomorrow you take Girl home."

Captain Allen might *send* her back, Mina thought, but she was not going. If the Rangers would not let her stay, she and Nakona would set out alone. Nothing was going to stop her from rescuing Amaya. Maybe she was beginning to believe all the talk about good medicine.

One of the Lipan guides, Chaa, spoke. *"Capitán* Will, Lipans no stay with Rangers if send away Girl-With-Hair-Like-Sun. She bring good medicine. Send away make bad medicine."

Captain Allen looked at him quietly for a moment before saying, "It's going to be bad medicine if anything happens to this girl."

"No have worry, *Capitán* Will," Chaa said. "We keep safe. She *Alemán* sister. We guard with life."

There was a long pause. Then Allen nodded his assent, and the Lipans started back to camp.

Nakona spoke to Mina. "I take care horses."

She gave him the reins and took her blanket roll from behind the saddle.

"Well, *Fräulein,* I have no choice unless I want a Lipan mutiny," Captain Allen said. "You wanted an adventure, and, by God, you'll have one. Now let's all get some sleep." Turning to the Rangers he said, "J. B., you take over Daniel's post for what's left of the night." Without another word he stalked back to the campfire, followed by Lieutenant Burleson and the men. Only Mina and Daniel were left standing by the river.

"You shouldn't have come," Daniel said quietly. "What got into you?"

74

Mina looked at him. His face was serious but not angry.

"Fire," she answered.

Daniel tilted his head to one side. "What do you mean?"

"Papa always says I have fire in my veins. I couldn't stand it any longer, Daniel, sitting at home, waiting and wondering." She looked down at the ground. "Anna says I should have been born a boy."

A smile came over Daniel's face. "I'm glad you weren't."

"Then you're not angry?"

"Nobody could stay angry at you very long, not even Captain Allen. Just don't cross him any more."

"No."

Daniel shook his head from side to side. "I don't know what is to become of you, Mina, with your different ideas, but I'm not entirely sorry you've come."

That made Mina feel warm inside, and she smiled.

The camp was quiet again. Dark forms wrapped in blankets like cocoons lay around the fire. To one side Mina saw where Nakona and the Lipans slept together. Mina and Daniel crept silently into the circle and spread their blankets beside a fallen tree. Mina took the five-shooter from her belt and placed it carefully under the tree trunk. Then she lay down and wrapped the blanket around her.

Overhead a dark canopy of leaves sheltered them from the vastness of the sky. Her mind went back to the canopy over her bed in Wehrstedt, Germany, which she had shared with cousin Christine. It was dark wood, and in the center Opa had carved a cluster of flowers.

Now she lay on the ground far out in the wilderness of Texas, next to the boy she loved, and tomorrow they would set out to find the Comanche village. This was the

75

adventure she had yearned for. Let others sleep in their cozy feather beds.

At first light Mina awoke to the sounds of the camp coming to life. The cocoons unrolled, and men began to move about at various tasks — kindling the fire, putting the coffee pot on, mixing a batch of biscuits.

She looked over toward Daniel, but his blanket was already rolled and lay beside his saddle. She sat up and saw that he had joined the men gathered around the campfire, sipping coffee, waiting for the bacon and biscuits.

After rolling up her blanket and tucking the revolver in her belt, she went off to the woods. When she returned, Captain Allen came toward her bringing coffee, a biscuit, and some bacon.

"How about some breakfast, *Fräulein?*" He was smiling. "You're going to need your strength today."

"Does this mean you have forgiven me?"

"No, but it means you can stay, God help me." He looked upward.

"I promise I won't hold you back."

Captain Allen sat beside her on the tree trunk. "That's not what's bothering me. You can ride as well as any man here." He glanced at the gun in her belt. "I see you brought along my old five-shooter."

"I thought I needed something." Mina bit off a piece of the crisp, warm bacon. Its salty flavor tasted even better than it did at home.

"Perhaps, but I don't want you trying to be some kind of heroine. You'll stay in hiding during our attack on the village. Understand?"

"But can I help rescue Amaya — somehow?"

"I don't know yet, *Fräulein.* We'll have to see what the situation is first."

That was good enough for Mina now. He had not said no. She took a bite of the golden biscuit and washed it down with coffee. "Good breakfast."

He nodded. "The boys do pretty well. You'll get your turn too, *Fräulein*. Happens this morning was J. B.'s turn to make biscuits. He's a surveyor From Tennessee. J. B. Walker. I reckon he's done a lot of cooking for himself."

Then Captain Allen pointed out each of the men who made up his small company. Besides Lieutenant Burleson and Ira Crenshaw there was Henry Starnes, who had walked all the way from Alabama with Buck McCauley, and Seth Cooper, a blacksmith. As he pointed out and named each of the men, some who were within earshot dipped their heads toward Mina in a rather gallant manner. "And I believe you already know the blond German." Daniel grinned at her. All in all, Mina felt more comfortable among them now.

"We're going to divide up this morning and search the riverbank for signs of the Comanche trail," the captain said, standing. "You'll ride with me, *Fräulein*, so get saddled up."

Mina picked up her blanket roll, found her saddle, and carried them to the spot where the horses and pack mule were tethered.

"Tucan," she said softly in his ear, "You and I must find the trail of your old masters."

12

Along the Comanche Trail

The Comanche trail had disappeared at the San Saba River. Chaa, the bigger and more talkative of the two Lipan guides, said the Comanches broke up here and took different routes.

Captain Allen decided to divide the men into two groups — one under his command, the other under Lieutenant Burleson — and search the riverbank in both directions. Mina, Nakona, and Chaa rode west with Allen and five Rangers, while the lieutenant, Batsosé, Daniel, and the rest of the company headed downriver.

Mina studied the ground ahead. More than anything she wanted to be the one to strike the trail. She searched for a hoofprint, flattened grass, or a dislodged rock, but she found nothing. It seemed the Comanches had vanished at the river, taking Amaya with them. Will I ever see her again? Mina wondered. What is she doing at this very minute? Has she tried to escape? These questions whirled in her mind.

The sun climbed higher in the sky and bore down hot on her back. Mina took off her hat and shook out her short, blonde hair. They rode through groves of trees, tall grass and wildflowers, and across rocks. The group had grown quiet, but locusts filled the air with their raspy songs.

After a while Seth Cooper said, "I reckon the Comanches have outwitted us."

"Looks that way," Captain Allen agreed. "It may be that we should give this up and head for the Colorado." Then he spoke to Chaa and Nakona, asking their advice.

Mina listened but kept her eyes on the ground. Chaa said the Comanches would cover their trail if they thought they were being followed. But Nakona did not think they would be worried this far into *Comanchería.*

The riders came to a low bluff where rocky ledges descended almost vertically into the river, leaving no bank to ride along. Tucan picked his way up to the top of the bluff as the men continued to talk.

This would not be a good place to cross the river, Mina thought. Unless . . . the idea came so fast it startled her . . . unless you were trying to elude your followers. Then it was the perfect place.

Mina nudged Tucan gently with her heels, and he pulled ahead of the other horses by a couple of lengths. She wanted to have a clear view all around. Concentrating on the ground, she no longer listened to the talk. Her eyes swept back and forth across the ground ahead. A certain urgency seemed to hold her attention and would not allow her to look up.

Then she saw something. A small clump of yellow flowers lay crushed on the rock. Her heart leaped.

"Nakona, look!" She pulled up on Tucan's reins, dismounted, and stooped to examine the plant.

The men stopped, their conversation abruptly broken off.

Mina searched the ground farther away from the river until she found a hoofprint in the sandy soil.

"It's the trail!" Mina said, looking up as Nakona, Chaa, Captain Allen, and the rest gathered around.

Nakona and Chaa studied the marks a moment, then followed the trail a short distance and found more hoofprints.

When they returned, Nakona said, *"Sí,* trail of Comanches. Girl-With-Hair-Like-Sun find trail." He had no expression, but Mina knew his face did not reflect his feelings. It hid them.

"You teach me, Nakona," she said in Spanish.

"Girl learn fast, have eyes like Lipan."

Mina looked at Captain Allen. Once again there was merriment in his eyes.

"Maybe Nakona and the Shaman know what they're talking about," he said. "Maybe you *are* good medicine for this expedition." Then Allen told Seth Cooper to ride back to Lieutenant Burleson with the news.

The men were in good spirits when they arrived. Gathering around the trail they marveled at her keen eyesight. Batsosé, Little Fox, looked at her with his sharp, black eyes, which did not seem quite so fierce as usual. In fact, they seemed almost admiring.

"Looks like you've earned yourself a place, Mina," Daniel said, dazzling her with his smile. "Where did you learn how to track?"

"Nakona taught me," Mina answered and noticed that his smile faded.

Before she had time to wonder about his thoughts,

Captain Allen said, "Well, boys, I think we had better get after this trail."

Nakona, Chaa, and Batsosé led the way, scouting ahead.

In the afternoon they came to a creek and stopped to camp. At Captain Allen's request the Lipans set out to hunt for supper. Others gathered wood or took care of their horses. Mina led Tucan to a grassy area near the creek where the horses were staked. She pulled off the saddle and gave him a good brushing. The skin on his shoulders twitched as she rubbed him down until his black coat shone.

The sun sank toward the horizon, but already the men had a good fire going. Captain Allen and Lieutenant Burleson sat on the ground studying a map. Daniel and

Ira melted lead over the fire for their bullet molds. Seth Cooper was busy constructing a scaffold for barbecuing meat, while Henry Starnes, the best cook in the company, stirred up biscuit dough.

Mina walked over to Mister Cooper and watched.

"Can I help?" she asked.

"Sure." His tight-set lips relaxed into a flicker of a smile. He handed her some branches and showed her how to lash them together with rawhide string.

Mina set to work, and by the time Nakona and the Lipans returned, they had the scaffold built.

Behind Batsosé, across the flanks of his horse, hung a doe. The Lipans laid the deer out on the ground, and Batsosé cut out the breast bone. He reached inside and took out the warm, steaming liver, which he lay upon a rock. Cutting it into several pieces, he put one in his mouth and chewed as blood ran down his chin. Nakona and Chaa took pieces, and Nakona offered one to Mina.

"You eat. It good for you." He held the raw, dripping liver out to her. "Eat," he urged.

As Mina shook her head she heard laughter all around.

Nakona threw the liver into his mouth.

Then Mina laughed too. "I still good Lipan?" she asked Nakona.

"Sí, you learn. Maybe mañana try liver, eh?"

"Maybe, if have much hunger," Mina said, hoping she would never be that hungry. The thought of that slippery, bloody liver in her mouth made her feel like gagging.

Amidst the laughter Mina glanced at Daniel and caught him watching her solemnly. He did not seem amused, and again she wondered. Could he be jealous of Nakona?

When the venison was roasting and dripping over the fire, and darkness lay all about, the men began to tell hunting stories as some smoked cigarettes. J. B. Walker told how his dogs had kept a bear treed all night until he came and shot it. Chaa told how he once thought he had killed a buffalo, but when he approached, the huge beast heaved to its feet and began to run. Chaa caught and held onto the tail, but all he got out of the chase was . . . At this point in the story he held up the tail. As Captain Allen translated, everyone laughed heartily, including Chaa himself. Even Batsosé had a silent grin on his face.

The firelight shone on Daniel's face. He was enjoying the stories, but he never looked at Mina.

13

Buhala!

For the next two days they traveled northwest, following the trail, going up onto higher and higher plateaus. With each rise the land flattened and fewer trees grew — only mesquites and occasional clumps of liveoaks. It was a vast grassland that dwarfed the small company of Rangers, three Lipan Apaches, and one German girl.

Nakona rode beside Mina, and Daniel stayed away, usually riding with his friend Ira. The distance that had come between Mina and Daniel made her miserable, especially out here on the lonely plains.

Sometimes Ira played his harmonica. Even though Mina did not know the songs — some lively, others sad — the music spoke to her without words. One song he played was a mournful melody that seemed to come from the wind sweeping across the empty land. She thought of Papa playing his harmonica in the evenings by the fire.

"Girl have tiredness?" Nakona asked.

Mina shook her head no.

"Maybe eat liver. Make strong."

She grinned but did not look at Nakona. Instead she glanced back at Daniel, waiting for the chance to talk to him and end this silent quarrel.

When Ira Crenshaw rode up front to talk to Captain Allen, leaving Daniel alone, Mina saw her chance.

"I talk with Daniel," she said to Nakona, and, without waiting for a response, held Tucan back until Daniel came alongside her. He kept looking straight ahead.

"I wanted to talk to you," Mina said to the side of his face.

Daniel said nothing, but his jaw clenched.

"What's wrong? Are you angry with me?"

"No." Still he did not look at her.

Mina noticed, though, that he pulled back slightly on Red Dancer's reins so that the horse slowed his gait. She did the same until they had fallen a short distance behind the group. Nakona glanced around once.

"Then why are you acting so strange?" Mina continued. "As if I'm not even here."

"You *shouldn't* be here."

"But you said you weren't entirely sorry."

Then he turned and looked directly at her with his blue eyes. "If you want to know the truth, Mina, I don't like the way you smile so prettily at Nakona."

"Why, Daniel Hessler, would you be jealous?" For a moment it seemed like their old bantering, but Daniel was serious.

He snorted. "Of a savage? No, Mina, I'm just warning you. Don't be encouraging him. Indians have a different way of looking at women than we do."

"He's only protecting me, as Chief Custaleta instructed him to do. Besides, he believes I bring good medicine that will rescue Amaya."

"Maybe, but he *sees* that you're a beautiful young woman — in spite of your short hair and boy's clothes and your medicine."

Mina felt herself blush. Still, it was better than being ignored.

"In fact, all the men here see that," Daniel said. "It's not proper."

That word always stirred her up inside. "You and *Tante* Lisette, always trying to make me into a proper lady. Well, I'll never be one. I thought you knew that."

"Then go marry some Indian warrior if you want, I don't care!" He left her and rode up with Captain Allen.

What a hateful thing to say. He didn't understand her at all — or didn't want to. Why had she been born a girl with fire in her veins, a girl who grew restless with sitting at home? She could not think why.

When she caught up with Nakona once more, they rode silently for a while.

Then Nakona said, "Girl-With-Hair-Like-Sun love Boy-With-Hair-Like-Sun, *sí?*"

"No!" Mina said, scowling, although she knew he was right.

"I think *sí*," Nakona added.

On the third morning a low bank of dark clouds moved slowly toward them from the north. As the darkness spread overhead, a brisk wind blew. The men put on their slickers and pulled their hats down securely.

A streak of lightning flashed out of the dark mass, and a sharp crack of thunder set the horses on edge. Rain began to fall in big drops. Mina untied her slicker from behind the saddle and put it on. Tucan whinnied and jerked his head around. She tried to soothe him, stroking his neck, but he would not be calmed.

"It's all right, Tucan, you have been in storms before."

Something else seemed to be agitating him and the other horses as well.

Captain Allen raised his arm to halt just below a rise. "We'd best stay off that rise and wait out the storm here."

They dismounted, and Mina held Tucan's reins, talking to him. Lightning flashed close overhead again and again as rain poured down on the huddled group. One crack of thunder was so loud it seemed to pierce right through her body.

Suddenly, Batsosé knelt and put his ear to the ground. He stood quickly, pointing to the rise, and shouted, *"Buhala!* Buffalo!"

Then she heard it, a low rumbling thunder that never stopped. Tucan pulled on the reins, urging her to go, to move out of the path.

"On your horses," Captain Allen shouted, even though most of them had already mounted.

Her heart pounding, Mina put her foot in the stirrup and swung up as Tucan sprang into motion. One of the reins slipped from her hand and dragged along the ground. He ran blindly with the other horses. Without warning, his head went down and he stumbled, throwing Mina over his neck, onto the ground.

She lay stunned for a moment as the rain pelted down, not understanding what she was doing on the ground. She felt and heard the pounding hoofs as the buffalo topped the rise and started down, crashing through small mesquites, trampling over everything in their path. Tucan struggled to get up. He lurched forward with a great heave and stood prancing about.

Mina scrambled up and took hold of his reins. "Come, Tucan," she shouted.

Lightning cracked close overhead. Tucan pulled back on the reins, jerking them through her fingers, but she held on. His eyes rolled wildly. Hand over hand she moved closer to him. He jerked away again, his reins flew loose, and he began to run.

The dark herd of buffalo thundered closer, their big heads lowered, short tails flying. Where was everyone? Mina looked about frantically, but it was impossible to see far in the pouring rain.

She began to run as two horsemen galloped toward her. One of them — it was Nakona — reached down, grabbed her around the waist, and lifted her up. Turning his horse, he held her securely in front of him. She got one leg over and held onto the pinto's mane.

Looking back for the other rider, she saw that it was Daniel. He fired his revolver into the stampeding herd that was bearing down on them. Abruptly the herd veered away from the three riders.

When Nakona had ridden safely out of the path, he pulled back on the rein and turned to watch the buffalo as they continued on southward. Mina shuddered to think she might have been trampled underfoot like the grass and scrubby trees. Her heart still pounded and seemed to rock her whole body as they watched.

Daniel pulled up beside them. "Are you all right, Mina?"

"I think so," she said, breathing hard.

Before she could say more, Daniel turned Red Dancer and rode back to the clump of liveoaks where the Rangers were gathered. Nakona followed him.

The rain had slackened, and Captain Allen stood waiting for them, a worried look in his eyes. He offered Mina his hand. Instead of taking it, she threw her leg over the pinto's neck and jumped down. She did not want to appear helpless in front of him. He might still decide to send her back with Nakona.

The captain's worried looked turned to amusement.

"I guess by the way you jumped down that you are not hurt."

"Only my pride," Mina said, still breathless.

He laughed then, and the men laughed with him.

Mina felt herself smiling and she looked up at Nakona.

"You save my life. *Gracias.*"

"I do what my father say. Keep Girl-With-Hair-Like-Sun from harm."

She owed thanks to Daniel too, but he did not seem to want any. He had dismounted and stood talking with Ira.

Mina looked about for Tucan and saw him standing alone on top of a knoll, off to her left. He was looking back at her as two Rangers approached him.

It had stopped raining, and Mina ran out to meet Tucan. Her little black horse walked along between Henry Starnes and Buck McCauley with his head low as if ashamed of himself.

When they met, Mina stroked his nose and then ran her hand over his slit ears. Tucan turned his head and studied her with his big, black eyes.

"He must have been scared by buffalo when he was still a Comanche horse," Mister McCauley said.

"It was my fault," Mina said, as much to her horse as the men. "I dropped the rein." As she mounted him, she said, "It's all right now, my little Comanche horse, it's all right."

Tucan whisked his tail and lifted his head as they trotted back to the others.

Captain Allen mounted Yack. "Let's get moving. We'll make camp at the next creek. Maybe by then the sun will be shining, and we can dry out a bit." Mina hoped so. Her denim trousers were wet through, and she was cold.

As they headed out, Mina edged over toward Daniel. Unwilling to let him pretend to ignore her any longer, she would say something to him. After all, he had saved her life as surely as Nakona.

"I saw what you did and I want to thank you."

"Oh, it was nothing," he said shrugging.

"No, it was quick thinking. And it was brave."

"Just as long as you weren't hurt, that's all that matters." Then he nudged Red Dancer and rode ahead, putting a distance between them.

Mina sighed. She could not think how to make things right again.

In the middle of the afternoon they crossed a creek running rapidly with reddish, muddy water. On the far side Captain Allen called a halt.

Chaa and Batsosé suddenly grew excited, pointing toward the northwest where buzzards were circling in the distance. It was a sure sign, they said, that the Comanche village was near. Mina wondered how they could tell it was a village rather than a dead animal. Perhaps because there were so many buzzards, and they continued to circle.

The three Lipans along with Lieutenant Burleson and J. B. Walker were promptly dispatched by Captain Allen to scout the village, the corral, and the whereabouts of the captives.

14

Plan of Attack

They set up camp under a big liveoak that grew at the top of a gentle slope down to the creek.

When the scouting party returned in the late afternoon, everyone crowded around to hear the news. Lieutenant Burleson said they found the village situated on a broad bend of the Colorado, about two hours' ride from here. There were eighteen tepees, and the camp was unguarded.

Mina listened, waiting to hear news of Amaya. Had they seen her? She could tell nothing from Nakona's face. He stood silently as Lieutenant Burleson, in his calm and unhurried manner, described a low wooded bluff opposite the village as being a good place to launch the attack.

The lieutenant picked up a stick and began to draw in the dirt. "Here's the Colorado," he said, drawing two parallel lines that made a big curve. "The village is here, and the bluff here, to the south. With the wind coming from the north, the dogs won't get a whiff of us."

"How deep is the river, would you say, Tom?" Captain Allen asked.

"It's quite shallow. Probably a couple of feet at the deepest."

Mina grew more impatient. She made her way closer to Nakona, and when there was a pause in the men's conversation, she asked him, "Find Amaya?"

He turned his face to her and grinned, revealing crooked teeth crowded in his lean jaws. "*Sí,* find Amaya and boy."

"She *bien?*" Mina asked.

Nakona nodded. "*Bien.* No have Comanche husband. Live with old squaw and boy in tepee by river."

Mina felt the tension go out of her body. Amaya was alive and well. Tomorrow they would see each other again.

Chaa drew circles on the map with a stick. "Tepees." He pointed to one close to the river at the east end of the camp. "Amaya here."

Nakona spoke to Captain Allen. "We have plan for take Amaya and boy."

"Tell it, Nakona," Allen replied, turning his full attention to him.

"Girl-With-Hair-Like-Sun put on dress of Amaya," Nakona said. "Make hair black. Go with Nakona before light to tepee of old squaw. Take away Amaya and boy."

Mina's heart leaped up. She could hardly believe what Nakona was proposing — that she steal into a Comanche tepee disguised as an Indian girl and rescue Amaya and the boy! Her mind raced along, and she saw herself entering the tepee, nudging Amaya awake. Would Captain Allen allow it?

"If old squaw see Girl in dark, think she Comanche girl, not worry," Chaa added.

Captain Allen was frowning as he turned to her. "Well, *Fräulein*, what do you think of Nakona's plan?"

"I will do it, Captain Allen."

He studied her closely. Then he picked up a stick and looked at the drawing in the dirt. "All right then. Here's the plan." He drew a circle for their present location. "At three o'clock in the morning we'll start out for the village." He drew a line to the Colorado River. "That should put us on the bluff, here, by five o'clock or earlier. Then you and Nakona will slip across the river. While Nakona stands guard, you will enter the tepee and bring out the captives. Meanwhile, Chaa and Batsosé will release the Comanche horses. As soon as you are back on the bluff, *Fräulein*, we will attack." He repeated the plan in Spanish for the Lipans.

Looking around at his men he said, "Our greatest advantage is surprise. It must be a complete surprise, boys. If . . ." he turned to Mina, "if there is any alarm sounded, we will have to attack immediately. Do you understand that, *Fräulein?*"

"Yes."

"That means you return."

"With or without the captives?"

"With or without," he said grimly. "I must have your word."

"I promise, Captain Allen."

"Good. Any questions about the plan?" he asked the group.

The men stood quietly. A few shook their heads no.

Captain Allen studied them, bringing his gaze to rest on Daniel and Ira.

"Now, you unseasoned warriors, this is your first In-

95

dian fight. I know how that feels — we all do. My advice is to take it one step at a time. Don't worry about tomorrow. Prepare for it. Clean your guns, get a good night's sleep. One step at a time."

He paused before going on. "I don't intend to lose a single man in this attack. The main thing is to keep your heads. Be aware of what's going on around you. We'll use our six-shooters first as we enter the village, at close range. Remember to hold back until I give the order to go, and don't draw your revolvers until you hear me shout 'powder burn them.' That clear?"

Daniel and Ira nodded.

"And that goes for everyone."

Mina wondered what Daniel was feeling. He listened intently to Captain Allen, but his face showed no emotion. Surely, she thought, he must be anxious about his first fight, but he would never admit it.

There could be no hunting and no campfire that evening. The Comanches must not be alerted. After an early supper of leftover biscuits and jerked venison, the men cleaned their guns, making ready for tomorrow.

Mina brought her five-shooter and sat beside Captain Allen. He knocked out the barrel wedge on his big six-shooter and removed the barrel.

"That's right," he said as she followed his example. "Now, you just push a damp cloth through the barrel like this." He used the wiping stick from his rifle and poked the cloth into the barrel. Then he dried and oiled it thoroughly and let Mina use his wiping stick.

The Lipans tested the trueness of their arrows by drawing them through their teeth, biting down to straighten the slightest bend. When Nakona was satisfied that his arrows were straight and true, he brought a small drawstring pouch to Mina.

96

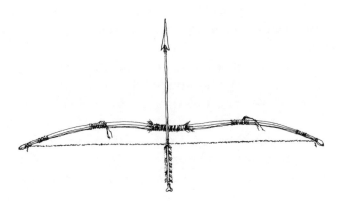

"You mix with water and put on hair. Make black like Indian," he said, handing it to her.

Mina opened the pouch. It contained powdered charcoal. In a tin cup she mixed the powder with a little water until she had made a thin paste. Nakona proudly produced a small hand mirror from his cosmetic bag and held it while she applied the black paint to her hair.

It went on quite easily. She moved this way and that to keep her image in the mirror. The girl that looked back at her — blue eyes, short black hair — hardly seemed to be Mina. *Tante* Lisette's words came to mind. *Like a wild Indian.* If *Tante* could see her now. The thought made her smile.

"Now you Girl-With-Hair-Like-Night. I not know," Nakona said as she finished the job.

Down by the creek Mina washed her hands and let her hair dry in the late afternoon sun. Then gathering her belongings she had spread out on the grass to dry, she walked downstream to a secluded spot where she could change into her Indian dress and leggings. Behind some brushy growth she removed her shoes, trousers, and shirt and pulled on the leggings. She slipped the doeskin dress over her head, fastened on her belt, and stepped into the moccasins.

When she returned to camp, Henry Starnes said, "Look here, we've got an Indian girl in our midst."

"Well, I'll be," Seth Cooper said. "You could of fooled me."

She glanced at Daniel, who looked at her strangely, as if he did not believe his eyes. Nakona and Chaa nodded their approval, and even Batsosé seemed to appreciate her disguise. A slight smile moved across his thin lips.

Mina began to feel like an Indian girl padding about in her moccasins. She liked the long fringe on the sleeves that swept across her arms. Looking down at herself, she remembered the day Wapako had given her the dress and said Mina had the courage of a Lipan maiden. She felt proud that Captain Allen trusted her to rescue the captives. She would not disappoint him.

As darkness settled around them, the men spread blankets on the flat ground under the big liveoak and lay down to sleep. Mina spread hers on the gentle slope overlooking the creek and slipped her revolver under the fork of her saddle. From there she could see Daniel's dark form sitting by the creek on first watch. She wrapped the blanket around her and lay back with her head on the saddle. Her right shoulder hurt where she had hit the ground when Tucan stumbled. She shifted to her left side and settled down for sleep. But her eyes would not close.

Tucan and the other horses cropped fresh green grass near the creek and occasionally snorted or stomped. And above, through the liveoak branches, stars glittered in the clear sky.

How quiet it was now with the men asleep. Only the

crickets played their pulsing song, and tree frogs called to each other back and forth across the creek. She yearned to go and sit beside Daniel and talk — not banter and argue, but tell each other their true thoughts. She was anxious about tomorrow. What if Amaya or the boy cried out when she awakened them? And what if something happened to Daniel? Mina felt a shiver go through her body.

She wanted to pour out these thoughts to Daniel, wanted him to deny that her worst fears would come to pass. But she could not disturb him. Captain Allen would be furious. He might even send her back home then and there — and for good reason. It was a fundamental rule that no one disturb the watch. The only worse sin was to fall asleep while on watch. The life of every person, including herself, depended on his being alert to the slightest sound.

So, she must try to sleep. They would arise long before dawn, and she would need all her wits tomorrow. Her eyes closed. It was comforting to know that Daniel was nearby, guarding the camp on the south, and Mister Cooper on the north. For tonight, at least, they were all safe.

Captain Allen had said he did not intend to lose a single man in the attack. She must think on that. *Not a single man,* she repeated over and over to herself. Slowly Mina sank into sleep.

Great shaggy brown shapes were thundering toward her. She began to run, but they came closer and closer until the warm breath from their nostrils enveloped her. Suddenly, she was at the edge of a precipice, and she plunged headlong over the edge. Down she fell, spinning around and around . . .

With great effort Mina struggled awake and sat up,

her heart pounding. A dream. It was only a dream. She blew out through her mouth in relief.

A waning moon had risen in the east, and she saw someone, she could not tell who, sitting on watch by the creek. Mina lay down once more, listening to the song of the tree frogs, and began to breathe in rhythm with them. It was a drowsy sound that lulled her to dreamless sleep.

15

Barking Dogs

Someone nudged her arm.

"Awake," Nakona said. "It is time."

Mina sat up with a start. Nakona arose and left her. Light from the half moon, now risen overhead, filtered through the trees, and shadowy forms moved silently about the campsite. For a moment Mina could not think why Nakona had awakened her in the middle of the night. Then she remembered. It was the day of Amaya's rescue, the day she had longed for. If only she could know how the day would end before it started. Deep inside her lurked a dread that something awful might happen. But she must not lie here and think on that. She must do as Captain Allen said, take one step at a time. And the first step was to get herself and Tucan ready.

Mina tied on her beaded belt and tucked the five-shooter in it. Wrapping her fingers around the grip, her thumb lightly on the hammer, she wondered if she could fire it at a human being. Firing at a target was one thing, but shooting at a person was another. She remembered firing Papa's shotgun at a Comanche lurking outside the cabin one night when Papa was away. But that was different. She had been inside the cabin and fired through a hole in the chinking. And she had not killed anyone, only frightened him away.

What if he had tried to break into the cabin? Could she have killed him then? The answer came immediately. Yes. And she could fire this revolver, all five balls, without any qualms. Besides, the Rangers said Comanches were not human; they were animals, savage animals to be wiped off the earth.

That resolved in her mind, Mina tied up her bedroll and lugged the saddle to Tucan, who was staked among the other horses. She set the saddle down on the ground and approached him with the bridle. He threw his head up nervously. Could he smell Comanches from this far away?

"Easy, Tucan," she said, stroking his forehead. "It's me. I won't let the Comanches take you back even if your ears *are* slit." Her voice calmed him. He turned his head toward Mina and nuzzled her hand.

All around the Rangers were saddling up or sitting astride their horses awaiting Captain Allen's orders. Mina picked up the saddle and laid it gently across Tucan's back. After tightening the cinch, she mounted and looked around for Daniel. With their hats on it was difficult to tell one Ranger from another in the darkness. As she searched, he rode up from behind.

"Take care of yourself, Mina." He spoke in German, his voice low, almost a whisper. His concern startled and thrilled her. He was no longer angry. His words wrapped around her, and she felt safe and warm.

"*Ja,* Daniel," she answered. "And you do the same." There was more in her heart, but she did not know how to say it.

He nodded once. "I will." Then he moved away.

Captain Allen mounted and wheeled his horse around.

"All right, men, you know the plan. Let's move out in two's. Chaa, *al lado de mí. Fräulein,* you and Nakona follow. Lieutenant Burleson and Batsosé bring up the rear. We'll maintain silence at all times."

Falling into procession behind the captain, they followed the creek to the Colorado River. There they turned north and rode along its bank. Through the trees Mina occasionally caught sight of the half moon swimming on top of the water. Saddle leather creaked and hoofs thumped the ground, but no one spoke. Their very success depended on being able to approach the village without being seen or heard. Several times she glanced over at Nakona riding so erect. Mina straightened her shoulders and felt the revolver at her side.

After a distance they veered slightly away from the river and rode until Captain Allen raised his arm for a halt. When Lieutenant Burleson and Batsosé had come up, the captain pointed to a liveoak in the distance. Underbrush grew beyond it, blocking any view across the river.

"The village is just on the other side there. We'll dismount under the tree and have a look."

Mina's heart lurched at the word *village,* sending blood racing through her body. The time for her to enter the Comanche tepee was drawing near.

In the shadow of the tree they all dismounted, tied the horses, and made their way through the underbrush toward the edge of the bluff. Across the river, clustered along the top of the embankment, were the pale, ghostly tepees, peaceful in the moonlight. In one of those slept Amaya and the boy, Max. Mina looked at the east end of the village to determine which one belonged to the old squaw. The one closest to the river — yes, that must be it. So peaceful was the moonlit scene that Mina did not want to think of the attack soon to come. She wished they could rescue the captives and leave the village be.

Captain Allen drew near Mina and Nakona and whispered, "Amaya and the boy sleep in the second tepee from the right, nearest the river." It was the one she had thought. "The entrance faces east," he added. Putting his hand on Mina's shoulder, he looked at her from the shadows of his eyes. "Remember, if the village is alerted, we will attack. In that case, I want you and Nakona to head for the river immediately and cross back here, with or without the captives."

Mina nodded her head.

"Are you ready then?" he asked.

"*Ja.*"

Her hand shook as she touched the revolver in her belt.

Daniel came over to her and said softly, "Don't be afraid, Mina."

"No." Even as she spoke her heart pumped faster.

"Fear makes you blind. You must keep alert."

"*Ja.*" She knew he was right. Taking a deep breath, she tried to calm herself. If they could just get started before she had any more time to think.

Nakona, Chaa, and Batsosé stood ready, awaiting Captain Allen's orders.

"All right, it's time to go," Allen whispered. "*Es tiempo para ir.*"

Nakona turned to Mina. "Follow my feet."

Mina nodded.

In silence they started slowly down the bluff, down through the tall grass and underbrush. Mina concentrated on placing each foot in Nakona's exact footsteps. She forgot what *could* happen and gave herself to the task at hand. Everything seemed suddenly clear and sharp — the dark form of Nakona ahead, the rush of flowing water. Even the stillness of the earth just before first light seemed stiller.

At the river's edge she did as the Lipans, removing her moccasins and wading soundlessly across to the other side. There they were hidden from the village on top of the embankment.

Without a word Chaa and Batsosé headed off to the right along the river. Nakona signaled Mina to wait while he crawled up the bank. She watched as he peered over the edge, his knife in hand. Then he motioned for her to follow. As they crouched in the tall grass, a few feet from the nearest tepee, snoring came from within. Mina's heart began to pound again. Inside that tepee Amaya slept unaware that Mina was so near. Who was it that snored? The old squaw?

Nakona stood then, and Mina followed him, circling around the tepee to the open flap. He looked inside and motioned Mina to enter.

She hesitated a moment, wiping her palms up and down on the doeskin dress. The sky was beginning to lighten in the east. Forcing herself to move, she bent and stepped in silently on her soft moccasins.

All was dark. She stood still, listening to the snoring, the deep breathing of sleep, and the throbbing in her ears. Gradually, forms began to take shape.

The snoring came from a large humped form to her

right, near the banked fire. The old squaw. To her left were two smaller, blanketed forms side by side.

She tiptoed toward them. Leaning close she saw the dark outline of Amaya's profile. Mina touched her shoulder. Amaya turned on her back and drew a sharp breath. Mina made the sign for sister.

Amaya started, peered into her face, and mouthed the word, "Mina?"

Mina nodded and pointed outside where Nakona stood guard. With a glance at the old squaw who still snored, Amaya touched the smaller form beside her. He slept on. She shook him gently, and he awoke with a groan.

The old squaw mumbled and turned her large hulk over. She sat up and spoke to Mina in a hoarse voice. Mina froze for a moment, not knowing what to do. The old woman seemed to take her for Amaya and was commanding her to do something. Mina dropped to the ground beside Amaya and lay perfectly still.

Satisfied, the squaw lay down. When she began to snore again, Mina and Amaya sat up. Amaya slipped on her moccasins and searched around until she found those of the boy. Then they stood and crept toward the opening, Amaya holding Max by the hand. Mina saw that she limped.

Suddenly, the squaw roused herself with a grunt and yelled at them. Before she could hoist herself up, they ducked out the door and, with Nakona, ran toward the embankment. In the dim first light, Mina glanced at Amaya and saw the pain on her face. As they started down the embankment, Amaya fell. Nakona swooped her up and carried her on his back. Mina took hold of the boy's hand, pulling him along. He made no sound.

Dogs began to bark — first one, then another and another. Splashing through the river, the four started up the bluff just as the Rangers, led by Captain Allen, came riding down to attack, yipping and yelling like wild Indians themselves. Mina scrambled out of the way and stood panting beside Nakona and Amaya, holding Max close to her.

16

When It
Is Necessary

Mina looked for Daniel as the company splashed through the river. Then she saw him next to Ira, leaning forward, urging Red Dancer up the embankment. His hand was on his revolver.

"Powder burn them," Captain Allen shouted.

Daniel pulled his revolver as they rode into the village. The first shots were fired, and she lost sight of him.

Please, God, let Daniel come out of this alive, she prayed silently.

Nakona motioned Mina to come as he started up to the hiding place. Mina glanced at the boy by her side. She had not really looked at him until now. His blond curly hair was matted and dirty. He wore only a breechclout, and there were cuts and bruises on his body. The boy looked up at her with alert, blue eyes, ready to do whatever she asked. He has spirit, she thought, or he would not have survived this long. Comanches had no patience with cowards. She wondered if he knew his father had been killed.

When they reached the top of the bluff and were safe behind some yaupon bushes, Nakona set Amaya down on the ground gently. She lifted one foot and removed her moccasin to show him. Mina gasped. The sole of her foot was covered with thick scabs. Nakona frowned as he knelt to examine the wound.

"Comanches burn feet so I not run away again," Amaya said in Spanish.

Mina stared at Amaya's foot and then looked back at her face as she replaced her moccasin. In spite of the pain Amaya smiled at Mina, and her dark eyes flashed with excitement.

"I never believe you here, Mina."

"I have to come. We sisters."

"Your hair . . . " She reached up and touched it.

"Black paint of Nakona," Mina said.

From across the river came the repeated sharp crack of the Rangers' guns and a confusion of yelling. Mina moved from behind the bushes to watch. Comanche warriors rushed out of their tepees, bows in hand, and stood firing arrows at the charging Rangers. Women and children ran screaming in terror. Dogs barked and occasionally yelped as they were trampled underfoot. Some of the Comanche horses scattered across the rolling plain to the north. Chaa and Batsosé had done their job. Warriors managed to catch others and mount them on the run.

Nakona mounted his horse and spoke in Spanish. "I go now. You safe here." He took his bow and one arrow from the quiver and urged his horse down the bluff.

Amaya stood beside Mina with Max between them. They watched as Nakona crossed the river and rode up the embankment, disappearing among the tepees into the jumble of people, horses, and dogs.

Max looked up at Mina and said, "I want to go home."

They were his first words, and as he spoke them, a tear came to each of his clear blue eyes and rolled down his cheeks. But he did not give in to crying. He looked steadily at Mina.

"*Ja*, Max, we are taking you home."

"When?"

"When the Comanches are beaten and chased off."

"They killed my Papa didn't they?" His dirty little face implored her to tell him the truth.

"*Ja*."

He leaned his head into Amaya and hid his face. She put her arm around him and patted his shoulder. Only a sniffling sound came from him.

"But your Mama is praying for your return. It will make her very happy to see you," Mina said.

He nodded but kept his face hidden against Amaya.

Mina turned back to the village, searching for a glimpse of Daniel. Comanches were scattering. Women carrying babies or holding children by the hand ran along the other side of the river. Warriors, some mounted two on a horse, fled from the village, firing arrows back at the Rangers and Lipans who took up the chase.

There was Nakona on his pinto, joining the chase. From near the river two Comanches riding together pursued him, coming up on his right side. One had his arrow drawn.

Amaya caught her breath. "Nakona!" She screamed some Lipan words that Mina could not understand.

A Ranger on a chestnut horse — it was Daniel — swerved over toward them, his arm outstretched. One Comanche fell to the ground. The other turned, his bow pointed at Daniel. As Mina watched, Daniel fell from his horse. The Rangers rode on in pursuit, and Nakona too, unaware that Daniel had saved his life. Red Dancer pranced about without a rider, but nothing moved from the place where Daniel had fallen.

Mina heard herself screaming Daniel's name and felt Amaya holding her back as she started for him.

"No, let me go. It's Daniel." She wrung herself loose and scrambled down the bluff, across the river, and up the other side. Her mind was empty of all but one thought that repeated over and over: *Let him be alive . . . let him be alive.*

The running fight had moved across the plain to the north and out of sight, leaving only the silent village in its wake. When she had scrambled up the embankment, Mina stopped and gasped. Crumpled forms lay about on the ground amongst the tepees. One of them was a child still clutching his toy bow, his face covered with blood. Nausea started up in her throat. Nearby a low mournful death song came from a warrior lying on his back, holding his chest where blood flowed from between his fingers. He raised his arms upward toward the sun for a moment, chanting Comanche words in monotone. Then they fell limp to his sides.

She put her hands over her ears and ran on beyond the village to where Red Dancer stood, his reins dangling. Daniel lay almost hidden in the tall grass with an arrow protruding from his shoulder. She fell to her knees beside him.

He lay on his back, grasping the arrow and struggling to pull it out. His eyes were clenched shut and he grimaced as he pulled.

"Daniel," Mina said.

He released his grip and looked at her. There was wildness in his eyes.

"Mina . . ." His breaths were short, quick. "Can you pull it out?"

She took hold of the shaft. Papa's words came to her: *When it is necessary, one learns to do what one has never done before.*

Mina pulled, but the arrow was firmly embedded in Daniel's flesh. Pulling again, she tried shifting it gently from side to side. Blood soaked his shirt. She remembered how Amaya had once shown her two kinds of arrowheads — one for hunting, the other for war. The one for war was barbed so that it could not be pulled out. The thought made her shudder.

"I'm afraid the arrowhead is barbed, Daniel."

"It has to come out," he said and began pulling on it again. More blood. "I can't breathe."

"No, stop, you're tearing up your shoulder."

He lay still a moment looking at her. "Then you'll have to . . . push it through." His eyes pleaded.

A cold pang shot through her stomach. Push an arrow into his body? There was already so much blood. She thought of the wounded Comanche back there in the village. She turned to look, but he lay still. Daniel must not die. Papa's words came again: *When it is necessary . . .* It *was* necessary now.

The sun was rising in a clear sky and shone down hot on them. He needed shade and he needed water. Mina looked around. Seeing a liveoak over toward the river she said, "If you lean on me, could you walk over to that tree?"

"I think so."

He sat up with the shaft sticking out of his right

shoulder. Then, ducking, she put her shoulders under his good arm.

"Ready?"

He nodded.

They stood together.

"Just over to the tree," she urged. He carried his own weight as she steadied him. Red Dancer followed behind.

As Daniel sat down and leaned back on the thick rough trunk of the liveoak, he was panting, grimacing with pain. Mina let him rest there a moment while she tied the horse. She picked up his hat where it had fallen and went down to the river for water.

Amaya and Max came out of hiding and approached the river slowly and, for Amaya, painfully.

"Daniel have arrow here," Mina shouted, pointing to her right shoulder. "I have to take out."

They crossed the river hand in hand as Amaya considered each step. When they reached the bank below the village, she called to Mina, "I look in tepee for to help." Max waited beside the river while Amaya went back into the old squaw's tepee.

Mina returned to Daniel carrying his hat full of water. She held it to his lips, and he drank thirstily. Then she began to tear his shirt away from the wound and made herself look at the jagged, bloody opening around the shaft. When she had removed his shirt, Daniel leaned against the tree watching her. His face was drained of color, making the blue of his eyes even more intense.

Amaya came bringing a pitch basket filled with fresh water, a buffalo robe, and a drawstring pouch.

"You save my brother, Daniel. Now we fix shoulder. I have good powder." She held up the small pouch.

Daniel nodded.

Max held a piece of blue cloth that looked fairly clean. He stared at Daniel. "Is he going to die?"

"No! Of course not," Mina said irritably.

He hung his head, and Mina was sorry she had spoken so harshly.

She touched his arm. "You can help us, Max. I want you to tear that cloth in strips about so wide and roll them up. And keep them out of the dirt. Can you do that?"

He nodded and began to rip the cloth.

Mina turned her attention back to Daniel. First she must wash the dirt and blood from his shoulder.

When that was done, there were no more preparations. The time had come, and she was the one who must remove the arrow.

She knelt beside him. His golden hank of hair slanted across his forehead, and she swept it back with her fingers. She leaned toward him and kissed him gently on the forehead.

"I love you, Daniel Hessler, or else I could not do this. Forgive me for the pain."

A smile tugged at the corners of his mouth. "Why, Mina, I could . . . die happy now."

"Don't talk about dying! I'm going to take out this arrow, and then nurse you back to health. Understand?"

Daniel nodded, the smile still lingering. He leaned his head against the tree.

With a fluttery feeling in her stomach Mina grasped the hateful shaft. She glanced at Amaya, who knelt beside her with folded bandages. Then, with one hand on his shoulder, she pushed the arrow in. It hardly moved. Daniel made no sound, but his jaws clenched. He watched her, never looking down at his shoulder. His steady gaze gave her strength. Again she pushed, this time firmly.

Her pulse pounded in her ears, and she held her breath. Suddenly, the resistance was over as the arrow broke through.

Daniel gasped, and sweat droplets stood on his forehead. Mina took the shaft in both hands and broke off the end. Then she pulled the bloodied arrow out as gently as possible. Amaya pressed the cloths to both sides of his shoulder to stop the bleeding. When they were soaked, Max handed her two more.

"Is it . . . out?" Daniel asked breathlessly.

"Yes!" Mina cried. "Yes, it's out." She felt light and giddy now that it was done.

When the bleeding had subsided a little, Mina bound up his shoulder. Amaya brought the buffalo robe, and they laid him down on it. Mina tried to smooth the crease between his eyebrows, but it returned as soon as she took her hand away.

Suddenly Max jumped up, shouting, "Comanche! Comanche!"

Mina's heart lurched as she pulled her revolver and swung around. Daniel lifted himself on one arm, struggling to reach his revolver, but he fell back exhausted. Amaya drew Max closer to her.

They faced a mounted warrior, his eyes fierce, his mouth grim. He had approached them unheard, and now the arrow poised on his bow was aimed at Mina.

17

Across
Two Cultures

Never had she seen such a fearsome sight. The warrior's skin was oiled, and the muscles in his arms gleamed in the sunlight. Hatred sparked from his black eyes. At any moment he would release the taut string and send the arrow plunging into her heart.

Mina cocked the trigger. Could he see that her hand shook, her aim wavered? She put her other hand on the grip to steady herself.

But as she sighted down the barrel, she saw the Comanche slacken the pull on his bowstring. He seemed to be studying her. As he looked at her with curiosity, his fierce expression slowly faded. He was no longer a wild savage with hatred in his eyes but a young man capable of other feelings, perhaps even tender ones.

Mina could not squeeze the trigger. She lowered the revolver as their eyes remained fastened on each other. He was a Comanche warrior and she a German girl, yet, in that moment, it seemed to Mina they were more alike than different.

He removed the arrow from his bow.

"Put away gun," Amaya whispered.

Mina slowly released the hammer. Her hand shook as she stuck the revolver back in her belt.

He spoke some Comanche words and made a sign, pointing at Mina and making a fist with his right hand over his heart. He pointed to himself, and with his open hand motioned from side to side in the sign for *no*. He drew back gently on his bowstring, the sign for *kill*. Then he turned and rode to the village.

Mina felt numb. All she could do for the moment was watch him go. He stopped beside the warrior who had sung his last song, picked him up, and lifted him across the horse.

As he rode away. Mina turned to Daniel. His face was pale, but his eye followed the Comanche. Amaya held Max in her arms, her head resting on his as Max looked at Mina with big eyes.

No one spoke for a moment. Mina was not sure what had happened just now. She turned to Amaya. "What say Comanche?"

"He say white Indian girl have strong heart. He no kill."

Only then did she remember she was dressed as an Indian. Though her disguise would fool no one in the light of day, could it have changed his mind about killing her?

"He spoke the truth," Daniel said.

"But I couldn't shoot him."

Daniel took a few quick breaths. "That took more courage."

Mina did not know whether it was courage or fear or . . . or a glimpse inside another person that kept her from pulling the trigger. But she knew that something had happened in that moment — something almost divine.

"If I had a gun, I would have killed him," Max said, startling her. He scrambled up and made a pretend gun with his fingers. "Bang, bang, bang, bang, bang — all five shots right in his heart. Then I'd cut off his scalp."

"Max, stop!" Mina said.

"But I hate Comanches. They killed my Papa. When I'm big, I'm going to kill every one I see." Tears began to stream down his cheeks.

"Maxcito," Amaya said, holding her arms out to him, and he came. She rocked back and forth, comforting him until his sobbing was over.

Meanwhile Mina turned her thoughts back to Daniel and the terrible hole in his shoulder. Could it ever heal? He sat beside her drawing shallow breaths, holding his hand on his chest. She looked at the blood-soaked cloth.

"We must change your bandages and put on some of Amaya's powder. Are you ready?"

He shook his head no and managed a slight smile, watching her as she unwrapped the cloth anyway. With dread she gently removed one bandage. The wound was like a gaping bloody mouth. A light-headed feeling and a sense of approaching blackness frightened her, and she took a deep breath and another. She *would not* faint and she must not let Daniel see her shock.

Dampening a cloth, she cleaned the blood from around the two jagged holes. Amaya shook the grayish powder onto two folded squares of cloth and held them over the wounds as Mina bound up his shoulder again with a long strip and tied it securely. Then she helped him lie down.

A horse whinnied from across the river, and for the

first time in hours Mina thought of Tucan, staked and alone on the bluff.

"Tucan must think I've forgotten him," she said to Daniel. She touched his cheek lightly. "You rest easy now while I go for him." Glancing at Amaya, she said in Spanish, "I go for Tucan."

The Indian girl nodded and moved closer to Daniel.

As Mina started toward the river she kept her eyes from looking over to the village on her right. But she could not keep her mind away. Her mind wandered amongst the tepees and stopped where the small boy lay so still on the ground. *Get up,* she said to him in her thoughts. *Get up and go play with your friends.* But he would not get up. He lay looking at her, his face covered with blood.

Mina began to tremble and tears blurred the bluff across the river. She had had enough — enough blood, enough wounding, enough killing. It was filling her up all the way to her throat. She felt heavy and tired, as though all her strength flowed out of her and into the river she was stumbling through. A sob came into her throat, and she covered her mouth. Why had she come to this place? Why had she left Papa?

Across the river she flung herself down in the tall grass and let the sobs erupt out of her depths until they were finished. Then, feeling a little better, she wiped her face on her doeskin sleeve and climbed up the bluff to where Tucan stood waiting. He whinnied again at the sight of her, and she flung her arms around his neck. "Tucan, I want to go home." He shook his bridle as if ready to go. Somewhat cheered, she untied him and mounted. He picked his way slowly down the bluff, and Mina relaxed, letting herself rock forward in the saddle with each step he took.

She looked out across the plain beyond the river. No sign of the Rangers. When would they return? She longed to have them all around, joking, laughing, making everything all right as it was before the attack. Would there be wounded among them? Or worse, had anyone been killed? Captain Allen said he did not intend to lose a man, but how could he be sure? She wanted Captain Allen here now. She wanted to start home. But most of all, she wanted Daniel well and strong again.

Tucan splashed across the river and up the embankment to the tree where Daniel lay. There was nothing to do now but wait. Amaya opened a parfleche bag containing jerked buffalo, pemmican, and dried prickly pear fruit. They ate hungrily. Daniel's eyes were closed, but he clutched his chest as he drew shallow breaths. The sun was straight overhead, and the katydids sang lazily. Mina felt drowsy. She lay down on the buffalo robe beside Daniel and sank heavily into sleep.

When she felt someone nudging her shoulder and heard a distant voice saying, "Rangers come," she struggled out of sleep and opened her eyes.

"Rangers come," Amaya said again, pointing out across the plain. Max stood watching.

Mina sat up and saw them, at first just a dark cluster surrounded by a cloud of dust. They came on at a steady, slow gait and halted near the tree. Mina did a quick count. They were all there, although she saw that Mister McCauley had a bloody bandage on his knee, and Samuel Ackermann's arm was bound up.

Captain Allen dismounted and hurried to Daniel's side. Lieutenant Burleson and the others crowded around. Amaya ran to Nakona and spoke Lipan words.

How good it felt to have the Rangers and Lipans back again, surrounding her, lifting some of the load from her shoulders. New energy surged through her body.

Allen turned from Daniel to Mina with a questioning expression.

"An arrow in the shoulder," she answered.

"And you pulled it out?"

"Pushed," she corrected, and shuddered visibly.

He looked at her for a moment and back at Daniel, who awakened with a groan.

"We're taking you home, Danny boy," the captain said. "Those Comanches are routed good and proper. We took a couple of hits, but we didn't lose a man — and don't intend to."

Daniel tried to smile, but each breath he drew seemed to pain him.

Nakona approached Daniel and knelt beside him. "You save life." He reached inside his medicine pouch and handed Daniel Mina's braid. It was frazzled but still held together by the blue ribbon. *"Iszeh inzoh,* good medicine, for you. Make well. Someday you marry Girl-With-Hair-Like-Sun, *sí?"*

Daniel's pale face flushed with color. *"Sí,"* he said quietly.

Mina turned away so no one could see her face. It felt hot, and tears started in her eyes.

"Well, now that Daniel's fate is sealed, let's get ready to start home!" Captain Allen said.

There were whoops and cheers from the Rangers.

"Ira and Seth," Allen went on, "you two devise a horse litter for Daniel. The rest of you set fire to the tepees and make sure no one is left alive. I want to leave a clear message if any of those savages return."

Without thinking Mina blurted out, "No, leave them be!"

122

She heard herself speaking the words as though she were outside her own body. "There has been enough killing."

For a moment Allen was stunned. Then he spoke quietly. "I'm not accustomed to a woman countermanding my orders, *Fräulein*. The fact is, any one of those Comanches would kill you on the spot if he had the chance, and burn your cabin to the ground."

"Not all of them, Captain Allen," she said, facing him squarely and on equal terms.

"What do you mean?"

"While you were gone a Comanche warrior came and threatened us with his bow and arrow. I pulled my revolver. But we just looked at each other. I cannot explain it exactly. It was as if I looked into his eyes and saw inside."

"And what did you see there, *Fräulein?* A human being?" Captain Allen laughed as did some of the Rangers.

"Yes," Mina said stonily, "and I could not kill him."

"You should never look into the eyes of your enemy, *Fräulein*."

"Maybe we *should*. He didn't kill me when he could have. I didn't kill him. Maybe we *should* look our enemy in the eye; maybe that would stop all this killing. I've had enough." Mina felt a welling up in her throat, and tears came to her eyes. But she would not cry. She clenched her jaws and looked away.

There was a long pause during which the only sounds were from the katydids and quiet shuffling movements among the Rangers. When Mina had composed herself she turned back to Captain Allen.

His expression had softened. "That's why there are no women Rangers, Mina. Comanches don't understand anything but force. They don't understand sweet looks and words."

"One did."

"I'm not going to argue with you any more. You've been through a lot today." A glint of amusement returned to his eyes. "But anyone who stands off a Comanche warrior deserves to have her way. So, we'll leave the village be, just for you, *Fräulein*." Then turning to the men he said, "Now let's get ready to move."

A small knot had clenched in her stomach. She would never learn to hold her tongue. No amount of Bible reading had the slightest effect. Could it be that she was *meant* to speak her mind? Did God intend her to do just that? What if she had not objected to Captain Allen's order? Perhaps there were times to speak her mind and times to hold her peace. That sounded almost biblical. She wondered if there was such a saying in the Bible, for it seemed to Mina that one could find a passage to support almost anything. She would ask Papa.

But what mattered now was getting Daniel safely home. All around her, men were making preparations to leave — eating cold food, filling canteens and water skins, reloading guns, and seeing to the wounded. Mina went to Daniel and knelt beside him. He sat leaning against the tree trunk watching Ira and Seth rig a litter for him out of a buffalo hide. They tied it to the saddles of Tucan and Red Dancer. Then they let Max lie down in it to get the horses used to carrying a litter.

"Can I ride in it?" Max asked as he wallowed about.

"You get an arrow in your shoulder and you can," Ira said and grinned at him.

On one side of Daniel, Buck McCauley sat unwinding the bloody bandage from his knee. On the other side Henry Starnes helped Mister Ackermann tie a new bandage on his upper arm.

"Just a surface wound," Starnes explained to Mina

as she watched him. "You did a good job on the boy here." He motioned to Daniel. "That took some courage."

"More on his part than mine," Mina said as she looked back at Daniel.

He held his chest with one hand and smiled faintly at her. "Quite a speech you made."

"I just want you to get well, Daniel. That's all that matters."

"I'll try. Just for you, *Fräulein*."

If he could still joke, there was hope, Mina thought. But it was a long, long way home.

When all was ready, Mina mounted Tucan. He turned his head to look at the strange thing attached to his saddle. He blew through his nose and twitched the skin on his shoulder to be rid of the thing.

Mina leaned forward in the saddle, talked to him soothingly, and stroked his neck. "You'll get used to it in no time, Tucan."

Then Ira and Seth carried Daniel to the litter. Mina on Tucan and Amaya on Red Dancer held their mounts at close rein. When Daniel was settled, Captain Allen gave the signal and they started for home.

18

Daniel's Delirium

Day after day they rode slowly across the rolling plains. Ira rigged a cover for the litter using another hide to keep out the hot Texas sun or an occasional spring shower. Frequently Mina leaned back in the saddle and over to the left to see Daniel's face. He passed in and out of consciousness as he was rocked and jostled between the two horses.

One night in camp something awakened Mina, but she could not tell what. She lay still, listening. It was a cool, overcast night. The wind soughed in the liveoaks that grew beside the creek.

Mina pulled the blanket up around her neck. She must have dreamed whatever awoke her. Unless . . . she froze with the thought . . . unless some Comanches had followed them. But either Ira or J. B. Walker would be on watch. No one could approach their camp without being heard or seen . . . unless the watch fell asleep.

She felt under the saddle for her revolver. The campfire still glowed, and she could make out the blanketed forms of men sleeping around it. Maybe she should awaken Captain Allen.

Just as Mina started to creep over to where the captain slept on the other side of the fire, the sound came again — a low moan and then mumbled words. It was Daniel. She hurried back to where he lay next to her blanket.

"What is it, Daniel?" She felt his forehead. It was burning hot.

"Mina."

"Yes, I'm here. Do you want water?"

He did not answer. His rapid breathing frightened her. She hated the arrow that had pierced his strong muscular shoulder. She hated the fighting that had brought Daniel to this. What if he grew worse in the night? And died?

Mina stirred herself, picked up the pitch basket, and poured water on a cloth to bathe his face. As she began, Daniel turned his head from side to side, mumbling words Mina could not make out.

"Wake up, Daniel, you're dreaming."

Suddenly he sat up, groping about with his good arm, uttering a rapid stream of slurred words.

Mina caught hold of his arm. What was he saying? She struggled to understand as he tried to free his arm from her grasp. Did he say something about home?

"*Ja,* Daniel, we are taking you home. Are you awake?" He quit struggling then and fell silent. "Here, drink some water." She held the pitch basket to his mouth, but he would not drink.

"You *have* to drink, Daniel, you have to," she urged, pouring a little on his lips.

He did not open his mouth or seem to hear her at all. She laid him back down on the buffalo robe. What could she do? For want of anything better Mina wet the cloth, squeezed it, and placed it on his hot forehead. It seemed useless. If only there were a doctor nearby, but there was no one for miles and miles, just darkness.

She remembered another time long ago on a cold windy beach, when Mama lay dying in a miserable makeshift tent. How helpless Mina had felt when Mama would not eat the broth she tried to feed her.

Now she felt that same helplessness. Mina put her hands to her face, covering her eyes. *Please God, not Daniel too.* She had never had much faith in prayer. Praying was good, she supposed, but it was not enough. Papa always said, *God helps those who help themselves.* But here, with darkness all around, she did not know how to help herself — or Daniel. And so she prayed. *Dear God, show me what I must do.*

Under a cloudy sky the wind swept across the grass and through the tree branches. She pulled the blanket up around her shoulders as she sat beside Daniel. He was quiet now, drawing shallow, quick breaths.

Then it came to her. She would sit here beside him all night keeping watch, putting cool wet cloths on his forehead. A sense of hope began to grow within her. She would not *let* him die. Leaning close to him she whispered in his ear, "You can't die, Daniel Hessler. You just can't, because I love you. Do you hear me?"

He stirred but did not answer.

She sat through the rest of the night, sometimes dozing, then waking with a start. In the east, low rippling clouds began to break up, catching the pink light of the sun on their undersides. Daniel had made it through the night though he slept fitfully. Mina lay down beside him.

128

When she awoke, some of the men had a fire going. She sat up quickly and looked at Daniel. His eyes were closed, his chest rose and fell with each breath. Reaching out from her blanket she felt his forehead. He was still feverish. Mina wet the cloth again and put it back on his forehead. It did not seem such a useless thing to do any more. It was something.

Amaya had left her bed on Mina's other side, but Max still slept, curled up under his blanket. Mina arose and went off to the bushes. On her way back she saw Amaya walking toward camp carrying something green. She walked gracefully now, no longer limping, with her long straight hair flowing down her back. Mina waited for her.

Amaya held up smooth pads of prickly pear with the thorns removed. "I cook — for Daniel."

"To eat?"

"No, to put . . ." She patted her shoulder. "I hear in night. Daniel have poison. This pull out."

"Truly?" Mina felt a surge of hope.

Amaya nodded, and together they hurried back to the campfire. The men were gathered around, drinking coffee, eating biscuits. Nakona, Chaa, and Batsosé sat on the other side of the fire, smoking sotol cigarettes, as was their habit.

Mina and Amaya placed the green pads on coals to roast.

"How's Daniel this morning?" Ira asked Mina, a frown creasing his freckled forehead.

"He has fever and was delirious last night."

"I heard."

When the pads were done, Amaya removed them to a flat rock to cool.

Captain Allen handed Mina a biscuit and a cup of coffee. "Eat, *Fräulein.*"

Mina took a bite, but the biscuit seemed to clog in her throat. She drank some of the strong bitter coffee to wash it down, feeling Captain Allen's eyes on her as she forcibly swallowed another bite. She must eat and be strong for Daniel's sake.

"We'll camp here for a few days to give Daniel a chance to rest," he said. "The men have agreed. And you look as if you could use some too."

She looked up at his serious deep-set eyes, yearning for reassurance. "Do you think he'll be all right?"

"I hope so. Indian medicine has its virtues."

As Amaya cut open the pads, she said to Mina, "Bring cloths."

Together, Mina and Amaya squeezed and scraped out the pulp onto the two folded cloths, making a poultice.

Daniel had not opened his eyes, but occasionally he mumbled. When Ira raised him up to a sitting position, his head slumped forward. Mina began to unwind the bandage. Suddenly, Daniel looked up. His eyes had a strange intensity, and he struggled to get loose from Ira.

"Hold on there, Daniel, it's me, Ira."

Daniel looked at him, his eyes staring.

"It's all right, Daniel, we're changing your bandage," Mina said.

He turned to her, but his eyes did not seem to see.

When his shoulder was uncovered, Mina caught her breath. His skin had reddened, and pus oozed from the wound. For a moment her stomach threatened to come up in her throat, but she took a deep breath and began to wash the poisonous secretions from his shoulder. Then she dried it carefully and, with Amaya's help, applied the two poultices, wrapping a clean cloth around to hold them in place.

"You see, Mina. Make well," Amaya said and smiled reassuringly.

They changed the bandage frequently that day and the next, making a fresh poultice each time. Daniel awoke and took some water. At last his eyes looked at Mina and knew her. He smiled weakly, drank the water she held to his lips, and lay back down to sleep. Mina watched him for a moment. His face, still flushed with fever, was turned toward her. She brushed his hair back and felt his forehead. It was warm but not burning hot. He *was* getting better, she thought, just as Amaya said he would.

Mina glanced around the camp and saw Amaya. She knelt beside Buck McCauley, spreading a poultice on his knee as he sat leaning against a tree. Her hair fell across her shoulders as she worked.

Mina went and knelt on the other side of McCauley's lanky, outstretched legs.

"How does your knee feel, Mister McCauley?"

"Oh, a little stiff, Mina, but I'll recover. Especially with such a good nurse."

"What about your patient?"

"I just came to tell Amaya that his fever is down a little."

Amaya looked at her, not understanding.

"Daniel *mejor*," Mina said.

"*Bueno*. I tell you. Make well, no?"

"*Sí*, make well."

The Rangers spent their time cleaning their guns, hunting, and smoking. Nakona and the Lipans straightened their arrows, repaired their bows, and plucked hair from their faces with shell tweezers. Chaa made a small bow and arrow for Max from oak branches and deer sinew. Then he taught him to shoot at a prickly pear cactus.

"Someday you shoot jackrabbits," he said in Spanish. Max did not understand, so Chaa put his hands to his head as ears and hopped about. Max laughed and began to hop about after him.

Mina busied herself making venison broth for Daniel. It would give him strength. And for the first time she could give thought to herself. After Daniel had taken some broth, she and Amaya went up the creek a way to bathe. Mina washed her shirt and hung it on a bush to dry in the sun. Amaya had soap made from yucca roots that foamed up into a lather. Mina used it on her hair as well, scrubbing until all the black color was gone.

That night Daniel awoke. "Mina?"

She was beside him in an instant and felt his forehead. It was cool and wet. His fever had broken. "I think you're going to live, Daniel Hessler," she whispered.

"I think I will," he said in a thick voice.

Mina gave him some water and lay back down, looking

132

up at the stars through the branches. Daniel would get well, thank God. They would go home. The very word sent a thrill rushing through her. What would Papa say? Would baby Peter run to her arms? Had *Tante* forgiven her?

In the morning Daniel was hungry. He sat up and ate some bites of venison and two biscuits. When Mina changed his bandage she saw that the redness on his shoulder had faded.

"Can you guess what Amaya and I put on your shoulder?"

Daniel thought a moment. "Buffalo dung?"

Mina covered her face and squealed with laughter.

Watching her, Daniel smiled. "Well, what then?"

"A prickly pear poultice," Mina answered, spitting out the *p's* and rocking back giddily with laughter.

How good it felt to laugh and tease with Daniel again. How good it felt to be going home.

19

The Gap

All afternoon they headed toward the same gap in the blue hills they had passed through on the way north. From there it would take two or three days to get to Willow Creek and home.

Mina and Daniel rode side by side, apart from the rest of the group. Amaya rode with Chaa on his horse today, giving Tucan a rest from carrying both girls. The sun was warm, and dust rose up behind them as the horses plodded along at a steady gait.

Mina opened the canteen she carried for Daniel and offered him a drink of water. His right arm was held in a sling. He grasped the canteen in the other, tipped his head back, and drank, his Adam's apple bobbing with each swallow.

Then, removing Papa's hat, Mina poured water on her head before taking a drink. Daniel watched with amusement as she shook out her hair in the sun.

"What are you thinking about when you look at me like that?" Mina asked.

"I was wondering . . . do you think Girl-With-Hair-Like-Sun would marry Boy-With-Hair-Like-Sun someday?"

A thrill washed through Mina's veins. Even though she had thought of marrying Daniel, he had never actually asked her. The suddenness of the question surprised her and, for a moment, left her speechless.

Then, just as suddenly, Mina blurted out, "How could Girl-With-Hair-Like-Sun marry? She doesn't have a dowry like a proper girl."

Daniel smiled. "Boy-With-Hair-Like-Sun does not want to marry a proper girl or her dowry . . . they could sleep on buffalo robes like the Indians. Besides, she *does* have a dowry, a fine black horse."

"And what if she wants to sail in a ship and see the world?"

Daniel laughed. "Well . . . I guess he would become a ship captain so he could take his wife along."

"He would do that?"

Daniel nodded.

"Then I say . . ." Mina looked at him, considering, teasing, ". . . yes, Daniel Hessler. Someday she will."

He grinned. "That's good enough for him." He put out his hand, and they shook on it.

What a curious way to propose, Mina thought, as if they were talking of other people. It was to her liking though, because she had not yet become the woman who would marry Daniel.

Nor was she the same girl who left Willow Creek looking for Amaya and adventure. She had found something more. She had found that she could do whatever she set her mind on doing, whether it was rescuing Amaya, convincing Captain Allen not to destroy the vil-

135

lage, or nursing Daniel back to health. There was strength in that knowledge, and she felt it coursing through her body. The kind of woman she would become was up to her, not up to the world.

Nearing the gap they came to a small meandering creek and stopped to drink and fill water jugs. When Ira lifted Max down from his horse, he ran to splash in the clear water. Ira walked over to Mina and Daniel.

"What have you two lovers been talking about?" he asked with a grin.

"Oh, just Indians," Daniel said, looking at Mina.

"I'll bet!" Ira dipped his hat in the creek and drank.

"We *were,* Ira Crenshaw," Mina said as she scooped up water and splashed him.

"Thank you, Mina, that feels good."

Lieutenant Burleson, who was still mounted, shielded his eyes and looked toward the gap.

"Captain!" he said suddenly. "A group of horsemen . . . there . . . coming from the gap."

Everyone stopped and looked. The horsemen made a dust cloud which carried off to the northwest and partly obscured them as they rode steadily toward the creek.

"Can't make out if they are Indians or whites," the lieutenant said.

"Mount up, men, and be ready," Captain Allen ordered.

Nakona rode up beside him. "Indian not make big cloud."

"I think you speak truth," the captain answered, "but I take no chances."

Mina squinted her eyes as she studied the group. If not Indians, might it be Papa? Her heart jumped up at the thought. She watched them coming closer. They had on hats. The man in the lead . . . "It *is* Papa!" Mina

136

shouted as she nudged Tucan in the sides. He splashed through the creek, up the bank, and out across a grassy stretch.

The riders halted as she galloped toward them, her blonde hair flying.

"Papa, Papa," she called, jumping off Tucan as she reined him in. He had dismounted. *Herr* Hessler, *Herr* von Trappe, and some others from Willow Creek were with him. So was Chief Custaleta. She saw them as she ran to Papa and flung her arms around his neck.

He wrapped his strong arms around her, and she felt him shaking as he whispered, "My *kleine* Mina." Her throat ached, and tears ran freely down her cheeks.

No one spoke a word, but she could hear the horses' hoofs and the squeaking of leather as the Rangers rode up behind.

In a moment Papa said, "Let me look at you, Mina." He held her by the shoulders. Tears brimmed in his big sad eyes and rolled down his cheeks into his fringe beard. His mouth was firmly set.

"Are you angry, Papa?"

"*Ja.*" He paused. "But happy too."

"Don't be angry, please, Papa. Look," she pointed to Amaya, "we brought Amaya home with us, and Max too, and Amaya and I nursed Daniel back to health. He got an arrow in the shoulder, and I . . ."

"You took it out?" Papa asked in astonishment.

Mina nodded. "You know, when it is necessary, one does what one has never done before."

Papa's mouth broadened into a smile, and his eyes shone. "Even if you are a bit foolhardy, Mina, I can't stay angry with you."

Daniel stood nearby talking to his father, who listened with a somber expression.

Herr Hessler put his hand on Daniel's good shoulder. "Now, you come home and be a farmer, my son."

"I'll do what I must, Papa, as you did when we came to Texas."

"So . . ." *Herr* Hessler said thoughtfully. "Do you mean to stay with Captain Allen's company?"

Daniel glanced at the captain. "As long as I am needed."

Herr Hessler nodded his head. "But you will come home and let your mother fuss over you for a while, *ja?*"

"*Ja,* Papa." He grinned.

Nakona and Amaya had approached their father. Chief Custaleta held himself straight, his face immobile. He nodded his head and spoke a few Lipan words, then handed Nakona Mina's other braid. Nakona took it, nodding once.

Captain Allen came to Mina and Papa.

"Thank you for bringing her home safely, William," Papa said.

Allen smiled. "She brought herself, Ernst. The Lipans believe she also brought us good medicine, and I have to admit that I agree." He looked at Mina, his eyes glinting.

"What do you mean?"

The captain spoke in Spanish to Nakona, who held up Mina's braid.

"Shaman say golden hair good medicine, find daughter of Chief," Nakona said. "He speak truth. He very old and wise."

Mina explained to Papa what he had said.

"Do you believe that, Mina?" Papa asked.

She thought for a moment. "I think if you truly believe in your medicine, it works."

138

Papa nodded, watching her closely as though he were seeing a new person.

Custaleta came closer. *"Muchas gracias,* Girl-With-Hair-Like-Sun, *Capitán* Will, for bringing home my daughter." He dipped his head, saluting them. "We have big feast and dance when return. Big feast for all. You come."

Captain Allen looked around at his men. Then, turning back to the Chief, he said, *"Sí,* Chief Custaleta, we come."

Custaleta looked at Papa. After Mina translated his invitation, Papa nodded yes and put out his hand. The Chief took it in his and they shook. Then Custaleta placed his other hand on top, smiling.

"We fathers of sisters. Make us one people," Custaleta said in Spanish.

Mina's heart went out to the Chief, and if it were not against his custom, she would have thrown her arms around him. She told Papa what he had said.

"Sí," Papa responded and placed his hand on Custaleta's in a final shake.

"Well, Mina," Papa said, "are you ready to come home? *Tante* Lisette and Peter are waiting for you."

Mina nodded yes. "I've had enough adventure — at least for a while."

"Then I guess you will not wish to go with me to Austin on a hauling trip." A wide smile spread across his face.

"Do you mean it, Papa?" But she knew he did, for Papa was not one to tease.

"Ja, it is something I promised myself if you ever came safely home. And now you have."

GLOSSARY

GERMAN WORDS

auf Wiedersehen (auf Veeder-zehen)	farewell, goodbye
Frau (Frow)	Mrs.
Fräulein (Froy-line)	Miss, young lady
guten Morgen (goo-ten Morgen)	good morning
guten Tag (goo-ten Tahg)	good day
Herr (Hair)	Mr.
ja (ya)	yes
jawohl (ya-vohl)	yes indeed
Kartoffelsalat	potato salad
kleine (kline-ah)	little (feminine)
kleiner (kline-er)	little (masculine)
nein (nine)	no
Opa (short for *Grosspapa*)	grandpa
Tante (Tahn-teh)	aunt
wie geht's (vee gates)	how are you

SPANISH WORDS

Alemán (Ah-lay-mahn)	German
al lado de mí	beside me
bien (bee-in)	well
bueno (bweno)	good
capitán	captain
es tiempo para ir	it is time to go
gracias (grah-see-us)	thanks
mañana (mahn-ya-nah)	tomorrow
mejor (may-hor)	better
muchas (moo-chas)	many

muy (moo-ey)	very
río (ree-o)	river
sí (see)	yes
vamonos (vah-mo-nos)	let's go

APACHE WORDS
(spelling phonetically adapted in some words)

buhala	buffalo
godiyileh	let there be strong medicine
iszeh inzoh	good medicine
nini	hello
shikisen	brother

ACKNOWLEDGMENTS

My husband Tom consulted with me on plot whenever needed, but especially on Friday nights at our favorite local restaurant, Kerbey Lane Cafe, where they let us sit all evening. Tom read every chapter of every draft, and he, as well as my sons Karl and Daniel, gave me criticism, praise, suggestions, and, most of all, encouragement to go on.

Gilbert Jordan, my father and emeritus professor of German at Southern Methodist University, checked the German words.

Edgar Perry (Jaa Bilataha), director of the White Mountain Apache Culture Center, taught me some Apache words and suggested names.

Graciela Guerra checked the Spanish words.

John McBride Jr. and Bob Norment at McBride Guns, Inc., gave their expert knowledge of Colt five- and six-shooters.

Dennis Sneed, our family doctor, took on an imaginary patient, Daniel, and consulted about his shoulder wound.

Carolyn McIntyre Shefelman, an expert horsewoman, helped me understand how it feels to jump a horse.

My cousins Lois Jordan and Billy Wayne Koock offered their ranch house and well-stocked pantry for our visit to the Texas Hill Country. And during that trip Pat Grote let us climb her neighbor's mountain to see the "smoke on the horizon."

Eve Williams, assistant director of the Natural Science Center Pioneer Farm in Austin, gave me a tour of the farm.

Ralph Elder and the staff at the Barker Texas History Center, University of Texas at Austin, were ever helpful.

The title was suggested by Marguerite Sutton, librarian at Northside Elementary School in Angleton, Texas. When I described the plot, she reminded me that on the last page of *Willow Creek Home,* Papa tells Mina that the fire in her veins has forged a spirit of iron.

And finally, the quotation from *The Sign of the Chrysanthemum* by Katherine Paterson was used with permission of Harper & Row, Publishers, Inc.

SELECTED BIBLIOGRAPHY

Denhardt, Robert M. *The Horse of the Americas*. Norman: University of Oklahoma Press, 1975.

Dennis, T. S. *Life of F. M. Buckelew, the Indian Captive as Related by Himself*. New York: Garland Publishers, 1977.

Fehrenbach, T. R. *Lone Star: A History of Texas and the Texans*. New York: American Legacy Press, 1968.

Goeth, Ottilie. *Memoirs of a Texas Pioneer Grandmother*. Austin: Eakin Press, 1982.

Greene, A. C. *The Last Captive*. Austin: Encino Press, 1972.

Greer, James K. *Buck Barry, Texas Ranger and Frontiersman*. Lincoln: University of Nebraska Press, 1984.

Jenkins, John. *Recollections of Early Texas*. Austin: University of Texas Press, 1958.

Jordan, Gilbert J., and Terry G. Jordan. *Ernst and Lisette Jordan: German Pioneers in Texas*. Austin: Von Boeckmann-Jones Co., 1971.

Maxwell, James A. *America's Fascinating Indian Heritage*. Pleasantview, NY: Readers Digest Assn., 1978.

Newcomb, W. W. *German Artist on the Texas Frontier*. Austin: University of Texas Press, 1977.

———. *The Indians of Texas*. Austin: University of Texas Press, 1961.

Opler, Morris E. *Myths and Legends of the Lipan Apache Indians*. New York: American Folklore Society, 1940.

Perry, Edgar (Jaa Bilataha). *Western Apache Dictionary*. Fort Apache: White Mountain Apache Tribe, 1972.

Ragsdale, Crystal. *The Golden Free Land: The Reminiscences and Letters of Women on an American Frontier*. Austin: Landmark Press, 1976.

Smithwick, Noah. *The Evolution of a State*. Austin: University of Texas Press, 1983.

Stone, Eric. *Medicine Among the American Indians.* New York: AMS Press, 1978.

Tunis, Edwin. *Indians.* Cleveland: World Publishing Co., 1959.

Webb, Walter Prescott. *The Texas Rangers, A Century of Frontier Defense.* Boston: Houghton Mifflin, 1935.

Wilbarger, J. W. *Indian Depredations in Texas.* Austin: Pemberton Press, 1967.